THE WALLS OF DELHI

THE WALLS OF DELHI

three stories

UDAY PRAKASH

translated from the Hindi by
Jason Grunebaum

SEVEN STORIES PRESS
new york • oakland

Seven Stories Press
140 Watts Street
New York, NY 10013
www.sevenstories.com

College professors may order examination copies of Seven Stories Press titles for free. To order, visit http://www.sevenstories.com/textbook or send a fax on school letterhead to (212) 226-1411.

Book design by J & M Typesetting

Library of Congress Cataloging-in-Publication Data
Udaya Prakasa, 1951- author.
  [Works. Selections. English]
  The Walls of Delhi : three stories / by Uday Prakash ; translated by Jason Grunebaum.
    pages cm
  ISBN 978-1-60980-528-9 (hardback)
  I. Grunebaum, Jason, translator. II. Title.
  PK2098.41.D33A2 2014
  891.4'3371--dc23
                                    2013050997

Printed in the United States

9 8 7 6 5 4 3 2 1

THE WALLS OF DELHI

THE WALLS OF DELHI

This story's really just a front for the secret I want to tell you — a secret hidden behind the story. Why? Well, what do you call what reaches your ears? Rumours, rumours, disguised as facts, but nothing but rumours. That's how things are, I'm afraid — like the appearance that I might disappear at any moment. Gone in my very own time.

The paan shop leads to the opening of a tunnel full of the creatures of the city, and the tears and spit of a fakir.

Sanjay Chaurasia's paan cart stood less than five hundred yards from my flat; Ratanlal sold chai right next to Sanjay's. Sanjay had come to Delhi from a small village near Pratapgarh, and Ratanlal from Sasaram. Their makeshift shops were on wheels so they could make a quick getaway in case an official came nosing around. Cops on motorbike patrol came by all the time, but they got their weekly cut. Ratanlal paid five hundred, Sanjay seven. The two men didn't worry.

'What's the big deal? I've got no problem. Say I did have a real place. I'd be paying the same money in rent anyway. Or more. Am I right? As long as a man is getting his daily bread, he can fight off the rabid dogs. When I'm right, I'm right,' Sanjay Chaurasia said, smiling. I wondered whose life was more like the dogs'.

A few steps away was a third enterprise on wheels – the bicycle repair cart belonging to Madan Lal. And across the road from Madan Lal was Devi Deen, the shoe repairman, and just down the road from him was Santosh, a mechanic who fixed scooters, cars, and repaired flat tires. Santosh had come to Delhi four years ago, making his way from a village in Haryana, close to where Madan Lal and Devi Deen were from. All the vendors and hawkers set up camp wherever they could. As night fell, Brajinder joined them, pushing his fancy electric ice cream cart, 'Kwality Ice Cream' printed in rainbow letters on the plastic panels. So did Rajvati, who sold hard boiled eggs. Her husband, Gulshan, was there too, with their two kids. Behind her shop, four brick walls enclosed a little vacant lot. As night wore on, people pulled up in cars asking Gulshan for a little whisky or rum. The government liquor shops were long closed by that hour, so Gulshan would cycle off and return with a pint or a fifth he secured from one of his black market connections. Some customers wanted chicken tikka with their hard boiled eggs, which Gulshan would fetch from Sardar Satte Singh's food stand up at the next set of lights. Sometimes, the customers would give him a little bit of whisky by way of a tip, or a few rupees. Rajvati didn't make a fuss, since it was a hundred times better for her husband to drink that kind of whisky, and for free, than to spend his own money on little plastic pouches of local moonshine. You could count on that kind of hooch being mixed with stuff that might make you go blind, or kill you outright.

The rickshaw drivers also hung around. Most of them came from Bihar or Orissa, and stood wearily amid the bustle on the lookout for passengers. Tufail Ahmed had come from Nalanda with his sewing machine, which he plonked down right beside the brick enclosure. He did a little business for a short while. But since Tufail Ahmed didn't have a fixed address, people were wary of leaving their clothes with him. So the only jobs he got were mending schoolchildren's bookbags, or hemming workers' uniforms, or patching up rickshaw drivers' clothes. After a couple of weeks, he stopped showing up. One person said that he was sick, another said he went back to Nalanda, and still others said he'd been hit by a Blue Line bus. His sewing machine was tossed into the scrapheap behind the police station.

It was the same story with Natho and her husband, Mangé Ram, whose cart was right next to Rajvati and her eggs. They sold channa masala at night and chole kulche during the day: no one had seen them for a few months. Someone said that Mangé Ram came down with stomach cancer, and that Natho had drunk away the money for medicine; and, after Mangé Ram died, she took the two kids, crossed over to the other side of the Jamuna, and took up with someone else who had his own kulche cart.

That's how it was around here, as if there was an unwritten law. Every day, one of these new arrivals would suddenly disappear, never to be seen again. Most of them didn't have a permanent address where you could go to inquire after they were gone. Rajvati, for example, lived two miles from here, near the bypass, with her husband and two kids, in sixteenth century ruins. If you've ever been on the National Highway going toward Karnal or Amritser and happened to glance north, you'll have seen the round building with a dome right beside the industrial drainage: a crumbling, dark-red brick ruin, with old worn stones. It's hard to believe that humans could be living there. The famous bus named *Goodwill* that travels from India to Pakistan – from Delhi to Lahore – passes right by that part of the highway.

But people do live there – families, for the most part, and two single men: Rizwan, whose right leg and hand have wasted away from leprosy, and Snehi Ram, who is so old that he sleeps all day long under the neem tree growing next to the sewage runoff. Snehi Ram knows the entire Ramayana of Tulsidas and the Soor Sagar by heart, and people swoon when they hear his rendition of the *Dhola Maru* and other epic songs. The two men can count on food handouts from the families living in the ruins. Rizwan gets up first thing in the morning, heads toward the bypass, drinks his chai and eats his bun at Gopal Dhandhar's, before installing himself at the bus depot until evening, begging. Rizwan's beard is streaked with grey, his face reminds you of Balraj Sahani from *Kabuliwala,* and he does quite well for himself.

Others live in the ruins: Rajvati's sister Phulo; Jagraj's wife, Somali, who sells peanuts by the gate of the Azadpur veggie market; and Mushtaq, who sells hashish by the Red Fort, and his cousin, Saliman, currently Mushtaq's wife. The three women turn tricks. Somali works out of her home in the ruins. She takes care of customers brought to her by the smackheads: Tilak, Bhusan, and Azad, who are always hanging around. In the evening, Saliman and Phulo go out in rickshaws looking for customers. Sometimes, Phulo also works at all-night parties.

Phulo occasionally sleeps with Azad, even though Rajvati, her sister, and Gulshan, her brother-in-law, both object. Gulshan always says, 'Don't lend money or your warm body to those living under the same roof.' Gulshan, Rajvati and Phulo have the most money of those living under that particular roof. Since Phulo came from the village and began to turn tricks, their income has increased so much that they've been scouting out land in the neighbourhood around Loni Border where they may build a house someday.

Azad says, 'If you move away, don't worry, I'll still manage,' but over the last few days he's been shivering and writhing around at night, sick. Gulshan says that he won't last much longer. All of the smackheads are in the same sorry state. Azad has the innocent face of a child, and is very light skinned. Tilak says Azad is the son of a rich family from Fatehpur. After his parents died, Azad's brother and sister-in-law took over the whole family estate. Azad's own brother-in-law was in on the deal, and got Azad hooked on smack – until it got so bad that one day he had to run away. Supposedly, he'd once been a real bookworm.

Azad and I had long talks, and he spoke quite articulately, even elegantly. I was amazed how much he knew about things like European perfumes and colognes, and their Indian counterparts, and horses, too; it seemed that he was fully knowledgeable about every topic, no matter whom he was talking to. His personality was perfect, apart from being a smackhead. But he'd been shivering these last few days, like someone with malaria or Parkinson's, and I had a strong premonition that one day I'd come visit, and Phulo or Tilak or Bhusan or Saliman would say, *What can I tell you, Vinayak? I haven't seen Azad for four days. He left in the morning, and never came back. You haven't seen him?*

And so the story goes with all of them. Azad wasn't coming back. What about me? I am Vinayak Dattatreya! Am I any safer than them? I've fallen to a new low, with no work, squeezed on all sides, and now I spend all day long sitting at Sanjay's paan stall: stressed out, useless, numb.

Now I'm just another piece of that world, no different from the rest. I don't have the courage anymore to come home and face the way my wife and son look at me. I watch my son eat his food at dinnertime, chewing ever so slowly, and I feel as though he's walking down a long flight of stairs, down into a darkness where I'll never see his face again. My soul – or whatever it is

7

you want to call it – quietly weeps. Believe me that every time I do a bit of soul searching to try and figure out what's wrong with me and why I have such bad luck, I come face-to-face with every single rotten thing about this whole system we live in – a system surely created by some underworld gang.

One day I'll be the one to disappear from this little corner of the neighbourhood: it's a fact. The poor, the sick, the street corner prophets, the lowly, the unexceptional – all gone! They've vanished from this new Delhi of wealth and wizardry, never to return, not here, not anywhere else. Not even memories of them will remain.

They're like the tears of an ill-fated fakir, leaving only the tiniest trace of moisture on the ground after he's got up and gone. The damp spot on the ground from his spit and silent tears serves as protest against the injustice of his time.

THE RUINED STATUES OF HISTORY AND THE GREAT COMMUTE
FROM CORONATION PARK

But it seems we've got off track. I was talking about Sanjay's, the neighbourhood paan shop (right near my flat), and then I got carried away to sixteenth century ruins near the bypass. But that's what happens. Try it yourself: look closely at anyone from a forgotten corner of any neighbourhood, and you'll slowly but surely find yourself entering a tunnel inhabited by very different characters. You'll notice that these city creatures are lodged in unfamiliar sorts of dwellings. But don't expect to read any news about the bad things that happen to them. Newspapers' *raison d'etre* is to hide that news, to edit out everything that they suffer.

If you're in Delhi, and you're the kind of person who doesn't sleep very well at night, and, at three or four in the morning, you're up, and you leave the house to go wandering around, then you've surely seen the road that goes toward Raj Ghat from Kingsway Camp, now called Vijaynagar. If you head toward Nirankari Colony or Mukherjee Nagar from the crossing at Vijaynagar, you'll find yourself in a desolate place that's known as Coronation Park. Even though they've turned the place into a big, beautiful park, it's the spot that gave the area the name of Kingsway Camp.

They say that during the time of the British, when George V or Charles came here (I don't know which one), all the Indian kings and queens of all of the princely states set up camp right there, gathering as one in order to warmly welcome their Imperial King. They say that it was a little like the reception that Bill Clinton got when he visited. The kings and rulers of the princely states performed a crowning ceremony, or the coronation of their English King. The speech that the King of England gave has been stored in the national archives, and the copy of the speech is considered a very important document in the history of India. On top of that, the King of England had a statue of himself installed slap bang in the centre of India Gate, under a lovely canopy. After the British returned to England in 1947, that statue, along with others dating from British rule, were uprooted, collected, and relegated to Coronation Park at Kingsway Camp.

In the years after Independence, the park became a magnet for loonies, beggars, the disabled, lepers, the maimed, druggies, and other wandering, unsettled individuals. They mutilated the statues, turning them into stoves, grindstones, sledgehammers, and using them in all sorts of other creative ways. A king's head was severed, a hand was taken, a leg removed. The torsos of the other statues lie scattered on the ground in a frightening, limbless state, surrounded by tall grass and shrubs. As soon as the sun sets, the special inhabitants of this park converge from each and every corner of Delhi, and pass the night among the felled, ruined figures.

So, as I was saying, if you're in Delhi, and things are such that an endless nightmare loops in your head all night long, and, in a fit of restlessness and depression, you go out wandering in the middle of the night, or right before daybreak, then you've seen them: the mass of human beings skulking out of Coronation Park, Kingsway Camp, loping toward Raj Ghat on Mall Road. The dark of the night hasn't fully dissipated, and dawn is still a hazy mystery, while you watch a great mass of broken, maimed, crippled, halfway-human beings, like characters from a Fellini or Antionioni film, as they quietly pass into the capital.

They're like a group of survivors of a devastating bombing campaign from a twentieth-century war, who pick themselves out of the rubble in the city that was the scene of the carnage, and carry their wounded bodies to a place of refuge, in search of a final protector.

After the sun comes out, you see them everywhere in the capital: at the train station, at bus stands, in temples, at holy sites, at intersections, on sidewalks. These are not the slum dwellers: they form their own constituency – one that's only got bigger since Independence.

In the corner of the neighbourhood where Sanjay's is, sometimes you'll also see one-eyed Rupna Mandal whose face is dotted with white spots from vitiligo selling colourful paper flowers and pinwheels. She, too, journeys from Coronation Park. Sometimes Sohna, a nine-year-old with no arms, another of the dispossessed, also comes along.

You see how this tunnel that starts from the little corner of the street that's home to Sanjay's paan stall leads to the Bypass ruins, from there to Kingsway Camp, and from there extends to each and every corner of the capital. Enter the tunnel, quietly make your way deeper and deeper, and you'll soon discover that the tunnel traverses the entire length of the country; then, it continues below the ocean floor, until, finally, it circumnavigates the entire subterranean earth. This is a different kind of globalisation, one so stealthy and so secret that not a single sociologist in the whole wide world knows a thing about it. Those who do know keep quiet, stay put, and wait until tomorrow. But the important thing to remember is this: the tunnel originates mere steps from my home.

Walk outside your home and take a good look at the little crowd that hangs out at the shop or stall or cart – and who knows? You might find where the tunnel comes out.

MEETING RAMNIVAS, AND THE START OF THE SECRET
It was at this little corner of the street I first met Ramnivas. He'd moved to Delhi twenty years earlier from Shahipur, a small village in Handiya district near Allahabad, along with his father, Babulla Pasiya. In the beginning, Babulla washed pots and pans in a roadside dhaba food shack on Rohatak Road, and was later promoted after learning how to cook in a tandoori oven. Five years ago, he built a makeshift house in Samaypur

Badli village in northwest Delhi, itself a settlement of tin shacks and huts – and just like that, his family became Delhites. Even though the settlement was illegal – city bulldozers could come and demolish everything at any time – he'd procured an official ration card after last year's election, and increasingly entertained the hope they wouldn't get displaced.

Ramnivas Pasiya was twenty-seven, twenty-eight, max. Ramlal Sharma, the local council man, put in a good word and got him part-time work as a city sanitation worker. His area was in south Delhi, in Saket. At eight in the morning, he'd put his plastic lunch tiffin, full of roti, into his bag, and catch a DTC bus toward Daula Kuan, and then transfer to another bus that took him to Saket. Ramnivas would punch in, grab his broom and other cleaning equipment and head toward the neighbourhood he was responsible for. When he got hungry in the afternoon, he'd buy a couple of rupee's worth of kulche, and then eat his fill along with the roti he'd brought from home. His wife, Babiya, had made the roti; they'd been married when she was seventeen. Now he was the father of two – a boy and a girl – and would have had two sons if one hadn't died.

I first met Ramnivas by Sanjay's. He had a good reason for frequenting the neighbourhood: he was chasing after a girl named Sushma. She was a part-time servant who washed dishes and did chores for a few neighbourhood households, commuting every day from Samaypur Badli, where Ramnivas also lived. Ramnivas had accompanied her several times, smoking cigarettes or bidis at Sanjay's or drinking chai at Ratanlal's while she worked. Sushma was seventeen or eighteen, a full ten years younger than Ramnivas. He was dark-skinned and lean – if the actor Jitendra were a little poorer, a little darker, and a little skinnier, you'd have Ramnivas. Sushma had a thing for him; you could tell just by watching them walk side by side.

The secret that I've been wanting to tell you is connected with the tale of Ramnivas. But please, promise me this: don't tell anyone who told you. You already know that I'm in way over my head, and if anyone found out, I'd be drowning in danger.

I saw Sushma just yesterday, and even today she came to clean a few houses in the neighbourhood. Every day, she still comes. Just like always.

But Ramnivas?

No one's seen him around for a few months, and no one's likely to see him anywhere for the foreseeable future. Even Sushma doesn't have a clue where he is. I've already told you about this kind of life: a man who you see every day can suddenly disappear, and never be seen again, not a scrap to remember him by. Even if you went looking for him, all you'd find – at most – would be a little damp spot on a square of earth where Ramnivas had once existed; and the only thing this would prove is that on that spot some man once did exist, but no more, and never again.

I'd like to tell you, briefly, about Ramnivas: a simple account of his inexistence that will reveal the first hint of the secret – the secret that these days it's vital we all know.

Two years ago, on Tuesday, 25 May, at half past seven, Ramnivas, as usual, was getting ready to go to work in Saket, forty-two kilometres from where he lives. His wife Babiya not only packed his plastic tiffin full of roti, but also placed a small metal lunchbox in his bag. In it was his favourite: spicy chole with vegetables, and aloo, too. Sushma was already waiting for him by the time Ramnivas got to the bus stop. Today, she was wearing her red polka dotted salwar, had used special face cream, and was looking lovely.

The previous Saturday, she accompanied Ramnivas for the first time on an outing to a movie at the Alpana. During intermission, they'd gone outside and snacked on some chaat-papri. In the theatre and afterwards, and on the bus going home, Ramnivas inched closer and closer to Sushma, pleading with her to say yes, while Sushma continually deflected his advances. After they'd got off the bus and were walking home, Ramnivas announced this before parting: if she wasn't at the bus stop waiting for him next Tuesday, it meant she wasn't interested, and they were through.

Now it was Tuesday. Every morning after washing up, he'd ask Babiya for last night's leftover roti, eating it before he left. This morning, he wasn't hungry, but weirdly nervous, and tried to hide it from his wife. His heart sank as he left the house, thinking, as he often did, that Sushma was having serious doubts. So when he saw her at the bus stop waiting for him, Ramnivas was so overjoyed that he declared they should ride in an auto rickshaw instead of taking the bus. He insisted and insisted, but Sushma wasn't persuaded. 'Why throw away hard-earned money? Let's just take the bus like we always do.' Ramnivas had fixed on the idea of sitting very close to her in the little back seat of the rickshaw, and maybe even getting a feel – and so he was crushed at her refusal. But Sushma's coming to the bus stop was a 'yes' signal to Ramnivas, and the man was beside himself. Now really and truly happy, he sensed that his life was about to turn a corner.

He was always picking fights with his wife, Babiya. Doing the housework and looking after the kids left her with no time, and one of the kids was always getting sick. Ramnivas could only remember one time (and he wasn't even sure of that) when he saw Rohan, his son, horsing around and having fun. Moreover, Ramnivas' pay cheque wasn't enough for Babiya to cover household expenses. Even though it wasn't her fault – she bought only what they needed – Ramnivas would let loose. 'It's like your hands have holes in them! Look at Gopal! Four kids, parents, grandparents, and god knows who else living with him, makes less than I do, and still gets by! And you? Night and day, bitch and moan.' She'd remain silent, but glare at him with a stare whose flames licked at the inside of his head all day long. That stare made sure he watched every penny. When he got hungry, he let his stomach cry out in pain. If he felt like chai, he did what he could to get someone to shout him a cup. He rode the buses all the time without a ticket. Babiya's burning stare, the one etched in his head, saw to it he never had fun.

That Tuesday, Ramnivas told Sushma he'd leave work early and be at Sanjay's by two, since that's where she'd be waiting; then they'd go home together. Sushma had said that she didn't like waiting for him at Sanjay's (Santosh, the scooter mechanic, was always trying to flirt with her, and Sanjay, too, was always cracking dirty jokes), but in the end, she agreed.

And then, for the very first time, Sushma, very slowly and very deliberately, instructed Ramnivas to bring her some of those chili pakoras, the ones he'd been going on and on about that they sell by the Anupam Cinema. When Sushma made her request, Ramnivas could swear he heard a note of intimacy in her voice, even a hint of possessiveness, and it made him feel very good indeed. He said casually, 'I'll see what I can do, let's

15

see how things go,' but had a very hard time concealing the fact that he was jumping for joy.

THE BROOM, THE GYM, AND MARS STARES AT JUPITER

Ramnivas went on his way, happy, while singing that song from *Kuch Kuch Hota Hai*. After punching in, he told his boss, Chopri sahib, that he needed to leave work early to go home because his wife was so sick she needed to be taken to the hospital. Even though he usually gave employees a hard time about leaving early and would insist that vacation forms be filled out, for some reason he readily agreed. 'Today's a lucky day,' Ramnivas thought.

That day, Ramnivas was sweeping the floor of a fitness club in a building that housed various businesses. Cleaning the gym technically wasn't his responsibility since it wasn't a government building, but Chopri sahib had instructed him to clean it, explaining to Ramnivas that rich people and their kids went there every day to lose weight.

The gym had every exercise machine imaginable: one for the waistline, another for the stomach muscles, and another for the whole body. The prosperous residents of Saket and their families went there in the mornings and evenings, spending hour after hour busy on the machines. A beauty salon and massage parlour occupied the first floor. Middle-aged men of means would go for a massage and, occasionally, take some of the massage girls back to their car and drive away. Ramnivas had seen policemen and politicians frequent the place.

Govind's chai stall was right outside, and he told Ramnivas

that a girl named Sunila earned five thousand for accompanying gentlemen outside the massage parlour. 'Who knows what these fucking big shots do with themselves in there,' he said. 'I've seen them throw after-hours parties, boys and girls right from this neighbourhood.' Govind did well during the late-night parties since the drinkers and partyers sent out for Pepsi and soda all night long. Indeed, while cleaning the bathrooms, Ramnivas sometimes stumbled on the kind of nasty stuff that suggested that someone had had a good time, and it wasn't much fun to clean up.

What a life these high-flyers have, Ramnivas thought to himself. They eat so much they can't lose weight. And look at me! One kid dies from eating fish caught from the sewer, and the other is just hanging on, thanks to the medicine. Then he remembered Sushma, that she'd be waiting for him at two at Sanjay's, and he set his mind to finishing up work.

As he was sweeping the floor of the big gym, the rope on the handle of the whisk broom that fastened the bristles together began to unravel, and he couldn't sweep properly. Annoyed, Ramnivas banged the head of the broom against the wall to try and right the bristles. *What was that?* Sensing something strange, he again banged it against the wall. This time, he was sure. Instead of the hard thud of a thick wall, he heard something like an echo. It was hollow, a quick layer of plaster had been applied, but what could be behind it? Ramnivas wondered. A table and chairs, and a couple of burlap sacks stood between him and the wall. Ramnivas moved them to make space. Then he hammered the head of the broom into the wall, hard.

It was just as he suspected. A few cracks began to show in the plaster, which soon crumbled away, exposing the inside. The strong smell of phenyl or DDT escaped. Ramnivas peeked in through the hole he'd opened, and his breath stopped short. He went numb. Holy cow! The wall was filled with cash, stacks and stacks of five-hundreds and hundreds.

He drew his face flush with the hole, and took a good look. The hollow was pretty big, like a long tunnel carved out on the inside of the wall. Nothing but stacks of cash, as far as he could see, all the way on either side until the light failed and the money was lost in the dark. Ramnivas' heart raced. His fear began to rise and he kept glancing around to see if anyone was there.

There was no one, only him, completely alone. Before him stood the wall in the big gym, at A-11/DX 33, Saket, against which he'd banged his broom and opened up a hollow, hidden space filled with a cache of bills.

'Dirty money… dirty money… dirty, dirty, dirty!' came the words, like a voice whispering into his ear. His hair stood on end. Here he was, face-to-face, an arm's length away from the kind of fantasy he'd only heard about from others. But this was no dream, no fairy tale, but the real deal. He'd stumbled on it, and here it was, right before his very eyes.

Ramnivas didn't move for a few minutes, trying to figure out what to do. Finally, he grabbed his bag from the table in the corner and, peering around to make sure there wasn't anyone watching, took two stacks of five-hundred rupee bills and stuffed them in his bag. Then he took one of the burlap sacks and placed it in front of the wall to cover up the hole along with the table and chairs. He hoped no one would suspect anything. Then he gave the floor a good sweep, cleaning up the dust and mess and plaster, and strode confidently outside where he plopped down at Govind's. He ordered a cup of Govind's strongest chai, and a couple of salty cakes.

'Yesterday was fine, but today – too hot!' Ramnivas declared. But Govind wasn't in the mood to chat: a government jeep had pulled up, and an order for five cups of chai and salty cakes came from inside.

'It'll get hotter,' was all Govind added, pouring the water into the pot. It was only half past eleven, and Ramnivas still had the better part of his cleaning rounds to finish. Instead, he went right to the office, hung up his broom, and said that he got a phone call alerting him that his wife had taken a turn for the worse. He needed to go home right away.

Each stack of cash contained ten thousand rupees, meaning that Ramnivas had twenty thousand. He'd never seen this much cash in his life, and was so scared that he rolled up his little bag and shoved it down his pants for the bus trip from Saket to Rohini. If any of his busy fellow passengers had had a moment to spare and had taken a good look at Ramnivas' face, they would have instantly realised this was a man in a state of high anxiety.

Ramnivas took a rickshaw from the bus stop to Sanjay's. He found Sushma joking around with the scooter mechanic, Santosh. This upset Ramnivas, but what unnerved him was when Sushma said, 'Enjoying a trip in a rickshaw today, are we? Did you knock over a bank or something?' But then she added, 'You said you were coming at two, and it's not even one. How did you get out so early?'

Ramnivas laughed. Maybe it was seeing Sushma, or just making it to Sanjay's – Ramnivas relaxed, his worries slipping away.

∽

A DREAM OF AN AUTO RICKSHAW, AND A SPECIAL TREE OF
PLEASURE

'I ran as fast as I could!' Ramnivas said, looking at Sushma with
a big smile. She returned his smile, but what Ramnivas said next
caught the attention of Sajay and Santosh, who suddenly looked
at him, causing Ramnivas to revert to his previous state.

'Can I buy you guys a cup of chai?' Ramnivas asked to a
startled Santosh and Sanjay.

'What's the special occasion? Did you get overtime?' Santosh
asked.

Sushma was also startled, since Ramnivas was known for
being such a penny pincher. She never liked the way he'd come
around Sanjay's and try every trick in the book to convince
someone to buy him a cup of chai, or a bidi. This day, however,
Ramnivas didn't just include Sanjay and Santosh in the round of
chai, but also Devi Deen, the cobbler, and Madan, the bicycle
repairman. And not just plain old chai, but the deluxe brew –
strong, with cardamom.

Sushma protested, 'why throw money down the drain like
that?' but Ramnivas didn't listen. He hired an auto rickshaw
for the rest of the day and took Sushma on a whirlwind tour
of Karol Bagh, Kamla Nagar, and Deep Market. He fed her
chaat-papri, splurged on bottles of Pepsi, bought her a handbag
in Karol Bagh, and a five-hundred rupee salwar outfit with
matching chunni from Kolharpur Road in Kamla Nagar.
Sushma, as if in a dream, felt indescribable bursts of happiness
each time she touched, or even looked at, Ramnivas. The sad
and worried little Ramnivas of yesterday (on many occasions

Sushma had thought, *enough is enough*) had suddenly blossomed into an uncannily happy, technicolour lover. Though his hair was unkempt, his stubble getting scraggly, and his bidi breath hard to take, whenever Ramnivas kissed Sushma in the little back seat of the rickshaw, for some unexplainable reason, she felt as if she were rolling around on a flowerbed of the prettiest blossoms in the world.

There's no way Sushma could have known what accounted for Ramnivas' surprising turnaround. She knew this much: She'd done well by showing up at the bus stand that Tuesday morning, after having spent the whole night thinking, *Do I show up? Do I not show up?* It turned out she'd made the right decision. *There is someone out there in the world who loves me!* Sushma thought, overflowing with joy. And she was with him at that very moment. To Sushma, Ramnivas seemed wide-eyed and innocent, like a little kid. Even a few days later after she began to sleep with Ramnivas, and even after he got her pregnant and then got her an abortion at the Mittal Clinic in Naharpur, she'd remember the whirlwind trip that day in the auto rickshaw. Two years ago, on Tuesday, 23 May, Sushma and Ramnivas had entered a fantasy land – the day Ramnivas found the cash hidden in the hollow wall of the building located at A-11/DX 33, Saket.

The roots of happiness lie hidden away in money. From there, the tree of pleasure can grow, and flourish, and bear the fruit of joy. Maybe the best qualities of men, too, lie locked inside a bundle of cash – this is how Ramnivas began to think. He was a new man: everything had changed. Gone was the poor, broken, sorrowful Jitendra. Now he was the gregarious, colourful, radiant Govinda, always ready to flash a smile. Life at home had also improved substantially. First, his wife, Babiya, seemed happy all the time, and cooked the most delicious food. They could afford to eat meat at least twice a week, and eggs every day. If he wanted to eat an egg, he'd go and eat an egg. The kids asked for ice cream, and the kids got ice cream. If a guest came knocking, Babiya would bring out the good stuff: Haldiram's namkeen snacks, and Britannia biscuits. 'Please, don't be shy! Why don't you take some more?' she said, offering the snacks on a fine little plate. Ramnivas bought a sofa, a TV, a VCR, a double bed, a fridge, a foreign-made CD player from Palika Baazar, and announced that it was only a matter of time before he bought a computer for the kids. He said everyone knew that in today's world, there was no getting ahead without one. He started looking into computer courses for his children, Rohan and Urmila. He planned to send them both to the States, where they'd work for a company and make six-figure salaries every month.

Ramnivas' relatives, who'd always steered clear of him, suddenly started showing up at his place with whole families in tow. Ramnivas, once decrepit and spiteful, now personified all the virtue and beauty the world had to offer, and Babiya wasn't afraid to sing his praise, all the time, and right to his face. His stock within his own caste community was on the rise, and he was often approached for advice about matrimonial alliances between families. He got all sorts of letters and wedding invitations. If he felt like it, he'd go. If he didn't, he wouldn't. But when he did – what a welcome he got!

'Take it – it's all yours. Don't worry about paying it back,' he'd be heard saying as he helped someone out. To paraphrase a popular saying, even a Ramnivas can get lucky.

Meanwhile, Ramnivas had begun drinking every day, and his liaisons with Sushma also became a daily occurrence. By then, Babiya knew all about the affair, but had decided to keep her mouth shut. She knew enough about the kind of man Ramnivas was to feel confident he'd never leave her or the kids. And so she didn't worry.

Sometimes Ramnivas wouldn't come home until well after midnight. Sometimes he'd disappear for a few days – sometimes with Sushma. But it didn't make any difference to Babiya: the neighbourhood now held Ramnivas in high esteem. He'd go straight to Sushma's house and had no qualms about talking to Sushma about going out to see a movie. Right in front of her mother, Bilaribai, who also washed other people's dishes and cleaned other people's houses.

Sushma now owned several salwar outfits, complete with matching sandals and jewellery sets. She used to go head-to-head with Ramnivas no matter how small the squabble, but now, fearing he might get angry, Sushma silently put up with more and more. On several occasions her mother cautioned, 'How long will this last? You have to stand up for yourself and tell him what's yours is yours. And *he* is yours, honey. People are beginning to talk.' But Sushma would reply, 'I'm no homewrecker, Amma. He has kids don't forget. Let it go for as long as it goes.' Deep inside she was sure it would go on forever, for the rest of their lives.

If people asked Ramnivas where he'd suddenly got so much money, he'd say that he'd got in on a half-million rupee pyramid scheme in Saket, or that he was playing the numbers and he kept hitting. Or that he'd won the lottery. Or – and this he reserved for only a few – that he'd met a great holy man near the mosque who whispered a very special mantra in his ear that caused future stock-market figures to flash before his eyes. In turn, Ramnivas whispered the same mantra into the ears of several people, all of whom failed to see the numbers flash before their eyes. Ramnivas explained that in order to see the numbers, one's heart must be pure. First you must bear no ill-will, prey on no one, cause no harm, and then you'd see: the market and lottery numbers would dance in your mind's eye!

Whenever Ramnivas felt like it, he'd go and fill up his bag with a few stacks of cash from the wall in Saket. It was amazing that no one had stopped him or arrested him, and no one had moved the stacks of rupees around. Spending the money as he pleased for so long with no one stopping him had turned Ramnivas into a carefree man, and so his daring grew. And yet he was still beset with worry that one day the rightful owner of the money might show up and take it away. So with wisdom and foresight, Ramnivas did two things to lessen the impact in case the money ever disappeared. First, he bought a ten acre plot of land in Loni Border, and put it in his wife's name. Second, he took three-hundred thousand and deposited it into various savings accounts in several banks, all under different names. One of them was a deposit of fifty thousand in Sushma's name, who had by then decided she wanted to go on forever with Ramnivas, just the way things were.

LOVE AT THE TAJ MAHAL, AN AIR-CON ROOM, EAGLE EYE, AND THE POLICE
It happened about eight months ago.

Ramnivas made big plans to take Sushma on a trip to Jaipur and Agra, where, of course, they'd have their photo taken in front of the Taj Mahal. It would be a fun getaway for a few days. Sushma instantly agreed. They travelled to Agra by train.

They found a taxi driver the moment they stepped out of the train station. Ramnivas instructed him to take them to a hotel. 'What's your price range?' the taxi driver asked, sizing him up.

Ramnivas could tell that the driver thought he was just an average joe, or worse, some schmuck. 'It doesn't matter so long as the hotel's top-notch,' Ramnivas said firmly. 'Don't take me to some fleabag, cut-rate flophouse.'

The driver appeared to be around forty-five; he had a cunning look on his face and dark eyes as alert as a bird of prey. He smiled, asking sardonically, 'Well, there's a nice three-star hotel right nearby. Whaddya think?' The man must have been expecting Ramnivas to lose his cool at the mere mention of a three-star hotel, but Ramnivas was unfazed.

'Three-star, five-star, six-star – it's all the same to me. Just step on it. I really need a shower, a hot shower, and a big double plate of butter chicken.'

The taxi driver gave him a long look, which he followed with a piercing, hawklike glance at Sushma. Pleased with himself, and now mixing in mockery, he added, 'Yes sir! On our way! And do you think I'm going to let you settle for a plain old hot shower? I'll see to it you have a whole big full tub of hot water! And butter chicken? Did you say butter chicken? I am going to take you somewhere they will serve you not just any old butter chicken, but whatever your heart can dream up!'

Ramnivas laughed at this and said, 'That's more like it! Now step on it.'

The taxi driver then asked, 'So where are you from, sir?'

'Me? I'm a Delhite. What, did you think I was from U.P. or M.P. or Pee Pee or someplace like that?' Ramnivas quipped, smiling at Sushma as if he'd just won the war. 'I come to Agra all the time. With the company car, every couple of weeks,' Ramnivas added, hoping that this shrewd driver wouldn't ask him about his big job. What would he say? Grade Four sanitation worker? Broom pusher? Janitor? But the driver didn't follow up.

When they got to the hotel, Ramnivas took the luggage out of the trunk. The driver told him, 'Go and see if they have any rooms. If not, we'll try someplace else.'

Ramnivas left Sushma in the taxi and went inside. When he got to the reception desk and heard the rate, he wondered if they should find a cheaper place to stay. But he soon signed on the dotted line for an AC room with a deluxe double bed for fifteen hundred a night. The man sitting at the reception desk sent Ramnivas upstairs to take a look at the room, and sent a bellboy on his way to fetch the luggage.

When Sushma arrived along with the luggage, she looked a little worried. 'Wow!' she exclaimed. 'What kind of a place is this, anyway? Everything's so shiny and polished, like glass. I feel like I shouldn't touch anything. What if it gets dirty? There's something about all this stuff, and the bellboy, too, that gives me a weird feeling,' Sushma added hesitantly.

After the bellboy had finished with their luggage, showed them that the pitcher of drinking water was filled up, and left, Ramnivas said to Sushma, 'Just enjoy yourself, and don't worry.

We've still got some stashed away, so why fret?' Then, lovingly, he added, 'Come over here and give me a big smooch. And crack open that bottle in my bag while you're at it.'

The knock on the door came at half past ten that night. It had already been a long day of sightseeing at the Taj, with all sorts of poses for the camera, then buying trinkets on the road, on top of which Sushma bought a set of Firozabadi bangles that had made her ever so happy.

Ramnivas wondered who it could be so late. He opened the door to find two policemen. One was an inspector, and the other, the inspector's sidekick.

'You've got a girl in there?' the inspector asked in a scolding voice.

'Yes,' Ramnivas replied. The inspector and his sidekick came in. The name *V.N. Bharadwaj* was engraved on a little brass tag pinned to his uniform. The way he was looking at Sushma! A fury began to build in Ramnivas, but he was too scared to say anything. Sushma was wearing her pink nightie, and you could see right through to the black bra he'd bought for her at Kamla Nagar. And beneath that was her fine, fair skin.

'Something tells me she's not your wife,' the inspector declared. 'So where'd you pick her up?' The inspector's square face housed cunning little eyes that kept on blinking. His hair had been turned jet black with unspeakable quantities of dye, and at first glance he appeared to be a sleazy, shrewd, thick-skinned man who liked to play by his own rules, and never ruled anything out.

'She lives next door. She's my sister-in-law,' Ramnivas said. He was a terrible liar. Between his fear and putting on airs, everything came out sounding feeble and wrong.

'So, you've been having a little party!' the inspector continued, glancing at the fifth of Diplomat on the table. Then he gave Sushma the hard once-over. 'She ran away. You helped her. You brought her here. My guess is she's under-age.' He turned to Sushma, 'How old are you?'

She was scared. 'Seventeen,' she said. For some odd reason she felt like something impossible was happening, and that she and Ramnivas would both perish because of it.

'I'm taking you down to the station – both of you. We'll find out from the medical reports exactly how much fun you've been having. That's a three-seven-five, three-seven-six, easy.' He pulled up a chair and sat down. 'So where'd the money come from? A three-star hotel? AC? My guess is this isn't your usual style. Did you steal the money? Or knock someone off?'

Ramnivas had a good buzz going, and should have been able to pluck up his courage; but Sushma telling the truth about her age had unwittingly thrown him to the wolves. He felt as if he was walking right into their trap. He thought quickly, and a smile took shape on his face. 'C'mon, inspector, just give the word. Another bottle?'

'That I can order from the hotel. As for you two – I'm taking you down to the station. Go on, get dressed. Is she coming like *this*? With her see-through everything?' the Inspector said plainly.

'What's the rush? The station goes wherever you go, inspector. The inspector's here, and so is the station. Why hurry? We can work things out right here,' Ramnivas suggested with a little laugh.

He was surprised at himself. Where had this been hiding, and hiding for so long? He took a quick look at the sidekick, who was standing by the bed, to see if he could get him to go along. It looked like yes, Ramnivas thought: The sidekick was busy staring at Sushma, but seemed to give a little nod when his eyes met Ramnivas's. 'Aw, they're just kids, Bharadwaj sahib,' he said. 'They come to see the Taj. Let 'em have their little party. You and me can have some fun with her too. Whaddya say, pal?'

Ramnivas didn't like what the sidekick was hinting at. On top of this debacle, Ramnivas was now becoming angry. 'Wait just a minute,' he said. 'Look, Bharadwaj sahib, as far as some food and drink go, just say the word, and I'll have it sent up in no time. But you've got to believe me that she's really my sister-in-law. I swear!'

The inspector began to laugh. 'Uh-huh. You need an AC hotel room in order to polish off a fifth of single malt with your underage sister-in-law? And then let me guess: The two of you were singing holy bhajans and clapping your hands? I can just see it. But now that you mention it, go get a bottle of Royal Challenge and order a big plate of chicken and some stuff to go with it. Actually, don't move.' The inspector sat down on the bed and said, 'I'll order from here.' He pressed the intercom button at the head of the bed that got him to the reception desk, placed the order, and then stretched out on the mattress. He loosened his belt buckle and regarded Sushma, who was sitting at the foot of the bed looking as if she wanted to crawl under a rock. 'And you – go sit in the chair in the corner and face the wall. Don't make me crazy. I lose it a little when I drink, and then the two of you'll go crying to your mothers about big bad Bharadwaj. I just can't help it, like when I see those pretty Western girls that come here on vacation.' He had a big laugh.

They killed the bottle in just over an hour. First, Ramnivas finished off his own fifth, and then joined the police in a few more shots from theirs — by the end, he was completely drunk. The inspector and his sidekick left the hotel room sometime after midnight. They settled on five hundred to let the matter slide; later, the sidekick shook him down for an extra hundred. By the time they'd gone, Ramnivas was utterly spent, and so drunk he was queasy and started getting the spins. Sushma helped him into the bathroom and poured cold water over his head, but Ramnivas lay down right there on the bathroom floor and began to retch. Out came all the butter chicken, the naan, and the pulao. After the vomiting subsided, he clung to Sushma, but everything was a blur, so he went straight to bed. He crashed face first, and in an instant a sound issued from his nose that seemed to come from the snout of a horse that had galloped from half-a-world away.

In the morning, Sushma told Ramnivas that after he got drunk he'd told the police about cash hidden behind a wall somewhere in Saket. Ramnivas instantly sobered up. He'd been so careful about keeping his secret! So much so that he hadn't even hinted about it to Sushma or his wife. In the end, a little booze had turned the sweet smell of success into a putrid pile of shit.

He made a few excuses to Sushma about something coming up back home, not feeling so well, and then canceled their trip to Jaipur. Ramnivas decided to take the next train back to Delhi.

Just as he'd feared, a police Gypsy idled in front of his house,
waiting for him the next morning. 'The assistant superintendent
wants to talk to you,' an inspector said from the jeep. He was
identified by the name embroidered above his breast pocket
as D. K. Tyagi. Ramnivas got into the Gypsy. As they left
Samaypur Badli, he saw the bus stop where he used to catch the
bus toward Dhaula Kuan, and where Sushma was waiting for
him today.

Some eight months earlier – I think it was a Tuesday – there
was a light cloud cover, and it seemed it might start to drizzle at
any time. That day, I saw Ramnivas at Sanjay's; he was waiting
for Sushma.

When the sky got overcast like that, and there was a trace
of drizzle in the heavy air, Ramnivas used to say, 'It seems like
the weather's whistling.' And when the weather was like that,
he'd take Sushma out for an excursion in an auto rickshaw and
feed her all the snacks and junk food in the world. But that day
something was on his mind, eating him from the inside. In half
an hour he'd done nothing but smoke one cigarette after the
other, and was biting his nails, clearly nervous.

I ordered two cups of deluxe chai from Ratan Lal, and got
my first inkling of how desperate Ramnivas was when I saw
him down the piping hot tea in one gulp, burning his mouth
and everything else.

It was early afternoon, and Ramnivas, eyes full of pleading,
looked at me and said, 'Vinayakji, I've got into a big mess. Way
in over my head. Help me find a way out – please! I won't forget
it for the rest of my life.'

I asked him to tell me all about it, and he did; and now I've told you everything he told me. When he finished, just as I was about to see if I could find some way to help – Sushma showed up.

'Meet me here tomorrow morning. I've got to go,' Ramnivas said, and the two of them jumped in a rickshaw. I watched them ride away until I couldn't see them any longer. That was the last time I saw Ramnivas.

He won't come back to this little corner of the street. He'll never come back. If you ask anyone about him, no one will say a word: not Sanjay, not Ratan Lal, not Devi Deen, not Santosh, and not Madan.

And if you keep going from this corner to the sixteenth century ruins at the bypass, and ask Saliman, Somali, Bhusan, Tilak, or Rizvan about Ramnivas, you'll get the same blank stare. Ask Rupna Mandal, the one-eyed girl who sells paper flowers and pinwheels, whose face is blanketed with white spots from vitiligo, or Rajvati and her husband Gulshan, who sell hard-boiled eggs at night – they'll all give you the brush-off.

Even the fair and graceful Sushma, who comes every day from Samaypur Badli to clean people's homes, will walk right past you at a brisk pace without so much as a word. That's how bad it is. Nowadays, she's been seen taking excursions in auto rickshaws with Santosh, the motor scooter mechanic. I saw the two of them munching on chat and papri in front of the Sheela Cinema last week.

That's how life goes on.

And if you happen to travel to that little settlement by the sewage runoff in Samaypur Badli and manage to ask for the address of the tiny hut that Ramnivas had converted into a real house, and, once there, ask his wife, Babiya, or his sickly son, Rohan, or his daughter, Urmila, *Where is Ramnivas?* you'll face a stare as blank and cold as stone. They'll say, *He's not home. He's out of town.* If you ask when he'll be back, Babiya will reply, 'How should I know?' and walk back inside.

In the New Delhi Municipal Office in Saket, where Ramnivas used to work, go and ask Chopri sahib or some other worker about a man by the name of Ramnivas, and they'll tell you, 'How are we supposed to remember the names of the hundreds of daily wage workers who come through here every day?'

No one in all of Delhi has any idea about Ramnivas – that much is clear. He simply doesn't exist anywhere – no trace is left. But hold on a minute. I'm about to give you the final facts about him. That's why I've used this story as a cover, so you can find the secret behind.

If you read any of the Hindi or English newspapers that come out in Delhi – say, *Indian News Express*, *Times of Metro India*, or *Shatabdi Sanchar Times* – and opened the June 27 2001 edition to page three, where they stick the local news, you'd see a tiny photograph two columns wide on the right side of the page. Below the photo, in twenty point boldface, the headline of the capsule news item reads: *Robbers Killed In Encounter*, and below that, in sixteen point font, the subheader: *Police Recover Big Money From Car.*

The three-line capsule was written by the local crime reporter, according to whom, the night before, near Buddha Jayanti Park, the police stopped a Suzuki Esteem that bore no licence plates, and was travelling on Ridge Road from Dhaula Kuan to Rajendra Nagar and Karol Bagh. Instead of stopping, the people inside the car opened fire. The police returned fire, and two of the criminals were killed on the spot, while three others successfully fled in the dark of night. One of the dead was Kuldip aka Kulla, a notorious criminal from Jalandhar. The other dead man could not be identified. Police Assistant Superintendent Sabarwal said that two point three million rupees were recovered from the trunk of the car, most of which were counterfeit five-hundred-rupee bills. It was the biggest police haul in many years. The Assistant Superintendent stressed the importance of information provided by the Agra police in netting the loot.

If you were to examine the photo printed above this news item, you'd notice that the car is parked right in front of Buddha Jayanti Park. The front and back doors are open. One of the men is lying face down next to the front tire, and he's wearing a Sikh pagri on his head. And the dead man lying right beside the back door seems to be staring up at the sky. Look closer – use a magnifying glass if you have one, or, better yet, enlarge the photo.

The dead man lying face up in the street next to the back door of the car, mouth open, pants coming undone and shirt unbuttoned, chest riddled with bullet holes from the police, is none other than Ramnivas – the criminal who, to this day, remains unidentified. And he will never be identified, since no one would recognise him any longer.

THE REVEALING OF THE SECRET, A CROWBAR, A TROWEL, AND AULIYA'S SHRINE
Now, listen to what happened that day, a few hours before the encounter.

According to Govind, who sells chai on the street corner in front of A-11/DX33, Saket, that night at ten, a police Gypsy came with three plain-clothes cops and two regular ones. They went into the gym, kicked out all the girls and boys who were exercising, and then, later, themselves left. About an hour later, as Govind was closing his stall, the Esteem pulled up. It didn't have any licence plates, and a Sikh, not too tall, not too short, got out.

Ramnivas stepped out of the backseat right after him. They went inside and stayed for about an hour and a half. They kept carrying things from the building and loading them into the back seat and boot of the vehicle. An undercover Ambassador car with concealed sirens pulled up right around the corner, where Khanna Travels and Couriers shop is, and followed the Esteem when it began to pull away.

Govind's shop was closed – he was getting ready to go home – when the greenish Esteem without licence plates pulled up right next to him. Ramnivas rolled down the window and asked for a bidi. Govind had an open, half-smoked pack of Ganesh brand bidis in his shirt pocket, and gave him what he had.

Govind said Ramnivas looked incredibly stressed, his eyes glazed over like those of a corpse. He'd tried to say something to him, but the Esteem was gone in a flash – the Sikh was driving.

If you're at Dhaula Kuan crossing and instead of taking Ring Road, take the next left, Ridge Road, you'll run into Buddha Jayanti Park. It's right off Ridge Road, and that's where the photo was taken.

According to what Ramnivas told me about the hollow wall in the gym at Saket, it must have been pretty large. Conservatively, I figured, it had to have enclosed an area of about twelve by four feet. Ramnivas had said the space was crammed full of one hundred and five-hundred-rupee bills. Based on that, I did the maths. What I came up with was that there was easily anywhere from a hundred to a hundred and fifty million rupees in there.

Do you remember the case where the Central Bureau raided a cabinet minister's house, along with a few of his other properties? The investigation was launched by the government that had just come into power, and the cabinet minister under investigation had been part of the previous government. The minister was charged with taking something like a billion rupees in kickbacks from some foreign company that supplied sophisticated high-tech equipment. The man did a little time, and was later released. He then joined the very same government that had earlier begun the investigation. It's clear that Ramnivas, guided by auspicious astrological alignments, or just dumb luck, had discovered a problem with his broom, and, in order to solve it, he began banging the broom head against the wall. He figured out the wall was hollow, put his hands inside, and was suddenly face-to-face with money hidden from the eyes of the Central Bureau and from the tax man. It was unaccounted money, untraceable money – dirty money.

Astrologer Pandit Deendayal Upadhyay set up shop to the right of Sanjay's, and just a few steps away from Madan's. He spread out his square of cloth on the sidewalk. I approached him and told him the whole story, changing what needed to be changed to remain discreet. The astrologer-ji told me this: If Jupiter, in the third house, aligns with Mars, while in the sixth house, Mars first aligns with Venus, then Jupiter, and then, by luck, it's the fourth or ninth lunar day of the waning moon, and a moonless night, and Delphinus is visible, then Kuvera, the god of wealth, will stir the senses of a man, and what this all adds up to is that there's a great likelihood of stumbling on some buried treasure, or major wealth.

Pandit Deendayal Upadhyay, originally from Baliya but now living next to the Naharpur sewage runoff in a rented tin shack, warned me. All planets and constellations were conspiring against me in the most dreaded alignment; Saturn was rising and casting a dark seven-and-a-half year shadow over my life, and I would soon face the full wrath of the government.

I think that Kuvera must have been in the right position last year, on Tuesday, 23 May, that made the change in Ramnivas' luck possible. Think about it: a simple whisk broom sweeps up the trash. The twine holding the bristles together gets loose, and the bristles need to be righted, so he beats the broom against what looks like a normal wall. And he finds a huge cache of cash. How? Think about it: for a few months he entered a fantasy land, getting everything his heart desired. He was able to give his wife, Babiya, and two kids, Rohan and Urmila whatever they wanted to eat and whatever clothes they wanted to wear. And he was able to take his teenage mistress to the other side of a shimmering, technicolour rainbow, where they got to see the Taj Mahal and have their pictures taken in several different poses.

That may be the case. But the astrologer-ji was quick to add that if the manna was, in fact, dark and dirty from the stain of sin, the result would be disastrous. What do I believe? I believe that somewhere around midnight on 26 June 2001, the sin, or vice, or bad karma attached to that money caught up with Ramnivas once and for all, bringing him and his dreams to a violent end.

And you ask me: so what's the big secret you want to tell me? Why use this story as a cover, and hide the secret behind it?

You already know that only a few lakhs of rupees were recovered from the trunk after Kuldip aka Kulla and Ramnivas were killed on Ridge Road that night – and a large part of that cash was counterfeit too. And yet, we know that there was at some point three billion rupees taken out of that wall.

The police officer who supervised 'Operation Ramnivas' is a respected and powerful cop who owns a few homes and has one of those farm houses outside Delhi perfect for all-night parties. And when he throws one, he invites politicians, high-ranking cops, journalists, top intellectuals, and a few senior literary figures. They drink until they fall down on the floor. I'm sure you've seen their photos in all the local Delhi papers. These people are no longer like you or me – they've helped turn each other into name brands. If you read any poetry or stories coming out these days, you know what I mean when I say that you can smell the stench of liquor coming from the words they write. And underneath their sentences lies a pile of chicken and goat bones, and the skeletons of the innocent ones. If you poke the head of your broom into contemporary literature, you'll find a hollow wall stuffed full of money – impure, dirty money.

I've been in Delhi for some twenty-five years, and I'm scared. I suspect that Ramnivas told the cops that he'd told me the secret about the hollow wall in Saket, and you know how much danger that puts me in.

It doesn't matter how many days I've got left in this sorry life before I also disappear – but I, too, would also like to enter into a world of my dreams, just like Ramnivas did.

So that's why every night at midnight, when all of Delhi is asleep, I put on some black clothes, sneak out of the house with a pick in one hand, trowel in the other, and spend the rest of the night scraping out the walls of Delhi. Treasures beyond anyone's wildest dreams are hidden in the countless hollows in Delhi's countless walls. I'm sure it's there, and I'm sure all of it is unmarked. My only regret is that I've wasted the last twenty-five years of my life. Even if I'd only taken twenty-five days to see what's inside the walls of Delhi, I'd be a billionaire by now, and I'd be able to live my life with a little respect.

So if you read this story, go and pick up a little pickaxe and trowel and get yourself to Delhi right away. It's the only way left to make it big. If you would rather live by hard work, the straight-and-narrow, following your dreams, using your talent, believing in yourself, keeping faith — if that's how you want to lead your life, you'll die of hunger, and the cops will never leave you alone. You probably don't know about that judge in Maharashtra who declared that the Indian police and the criminals and goons of the land are one big lawful family.

In the meantime, I'll settle down with the beggars, the lepers, the smackheads, the transients, and the other forgotten ones, I'll stretch out, and sleep among the dismembered statues of the old English rulers that lie scattered in Coronation Park. I'm broken in the same places, with my bad back and bone tuberculosis. Whenever I have free time, I go to the shrine of Hazarat Nizzamuddin, just past the Delhi Zoo, and sit for hours on the marble floor of the dargah, repeating the words that the sufi saint, Auliya – Hazarat Nizzumaddin – once spoke to the then ruler of Delhi, Ghayasuddin Tughluq. *Delhi is still far away.* Tughluq summoned Auliya to explain why the sufi saint was visited by more people than was Tughluq's court. *Delhi is still far away.* Auliya declined the summons, just as he had with all the other kings he'd seen come and go. *Delhi is still far away.* Tughluq left on a military campaign in the south to let Auliya think it over. *Delhi is still far away.* Auliya's followers warned him to leave Delhi; Tughluq had threatened to behead Auliya if he disobeyed the summons. *Delhi is still far away.* The night before returning to Delhi, Tughluq and his men set up camp just outside the city. *Delhi is still far away.* That's the night Auliya uttered the sentence I keep on repeating. After he spoke it, Tughluq, drinking and carousing, died right at the Delhi border when the tent he was in collapsed. That place is now known as Tughluqabad.

Amir Khusaro's tomb is also at Auliya's shrine – the man who wrote the first lines of poetry in what we now call Hindi – and who, in his own lifetime saw eleven kings, their courts, and their hangers-on, all come and go. If you go and look at the guest book that Sayid Nizami keeps at the shrine, you'll see my name.

Believe me when I say that I am praying not only for me, but for the well-being of all of you, and for that of my dear country. Have faith that my prayers will reach all the way to Auliya's ears.

So long as the police or other powers-that-be in this city don't frame me for something, I'll use my pickaxe and trowel to find the wealth hidden in Delhi's countless walled hollows.

And if you want to get lucky, come to Delhi right away – it's not far at all. Forget about being a millionaire; coming to Delhi is the only way left to scrape by.

The other ways you read about in the papers, and see on TV, are rumours and lies, nothing more.

MOHANDAS

For comrade Virendra Soni,
with the hope that he will stand
with Mohandas 'til the end

'[T]the most glaring tendency of the British Government system of high class education has been the virtual monopoly of all higher offices under them by the Brahmins.'

(Mahatma Jotirao Phule, 'Slavery')

'The British... validated Brahmin authority by employing, almost exclusively, Brahmins as their clerks and assistants.'

(Arthur Bonner, *Democracy in India: a Hollow Shell*)

What is the colour of fear? Is it the colour of dirt, or of stone? Is it yellow, charcoal? Or the colour of ash left over from a burning coal – ash that coats the coal still glowing red-hot, that still has its heat! Or a colour that masks a terrifying silence behind it? A small tear that exposes a frightful scream suspended behind.

Have you ever seen the bloodshot, dying eyes of a fish thrown from an ocean or a river, onto a sandy bank or shore? That's the colour.

The most talented actor, no matter how hard he tries, can't quite make the whites of his eyes or his pupils imitate the colour you see in the face of a living, breathing man who is scared clear out of his wits. Like a man going home after a hard day's work, exhausted, satchel in hand, penny candy and cheap toys for his kids in the bag, along with a few pills for his wife's cough. The man turns the corner into a deserted alley to find himself caught in the middle of a riot – and, unfortunately for him, he's the wrong religion or race as far as the gang or mob that's surrounding him is concerned.

The look in the doomed man's eyes, on his face, the posture of his body right at that moment, just a second or two before his murder – that's the colour I'm talking about, and that was the colour of Mohandas' face that day.

I'm sure you've seen films like Schindler's List or others that show German trains being sent somewhere far away. You remember the faces of the Jewish women, children, and the old men, pressed up against the insides of the railway cars, peering out. Or, more recently, the faces of those looking out from windows and rooftops in the cities and towns of Gujarat.

That's the colour.

'Is there any way you can get me out of this, uncle, please!' Mohandas stood in front of me pleading in a weak, wavering voice. 'I'm begging you, think of my kids, my father's dying of TB, just give the word and I'm ready to go to court right away and sign a sworn statement that I am not Mohandas. I don't know anyone by that name. Just help get me out of this!'

The first thing you'll feel when you look at Mohandas is pity, but soon you'll also feel fear. It's a frightening time, and people are getting more and more fearful every day.

I've known Mohandas for a long time, along with several generations of his family. That's how it is in little villages like ours. You wouldn't guess by looking at him that he was a graduate of our government M. G. Degree College, located right here in the Anuppur district, or that he graduated at the very top of his class; ten years ago, his name was number two on the list of the University's 'toppers'. The way he looked now gave no indication whatsoever of his past. He wore a torn, patched-up, washed-out pair of denim pants that had once been blue, and a cheap poly blend shirt with a frayed right sleeve. The faintest trace of a checked pattern remained on the shirt, but the lines had long since vanished. His cheap rubber shoes had been so ravaged by mud, dirt, misery, time, water, and sun that they sometimes looked as if they were made from clay, other times from skin.

Mohandas is probably around forty-five, but he looks as if he's at least my age or older.

I found him discombobulated, in the grip of terror. I had never seen him idling in the village, shooting the breeze, playing cards, or sitting around watching TV. He was driven by a kind of harrowing restlessness that wouldn't let him sit still for a second. People said he always found something to keep him busy, some job or chore. He needed to dig a new well every day for his water, and plant a new crop of wheat every day for his bread. And it wasn't just one member of his family he had to provide food for – there were five, five mouths and five stomachs. Mohandas's father was Kabadas, who'd been suffering from TB for eight years. His mother Putlibai had gone blind after a cataract operation she'd had at a free eye clinic, and now saw nothing but darkness. His wife Kasturibai was a mirror image of her husband: she helped Mohandas with his work, and kept the stove warm at home. The people in the village claimed the two had never been seen fighting or quarrelling. It seemed there had been nothing but trials and tribulations for husband and wife – things that either strengthen or weaken a union between a man and a woman.

Devdas is one of the two remaining people, and Sharda the other. Mohandas and Kasturi had two offspring. One was eight, the other six. Devdas went to primary school in the village; after school he worked as a helper at Durga Auto Works on the town bypass road, where he put air in tires, fixed flat ones, and did minor repair work on scooters and motorcycles. For this he earned a hundred rupees a month. In other words,

Mohandas's son Devdas, through his own hard work, took care of feeding himself while he was at school; he was self-sufficient. The teachers at his school said he was one of the brightest kids in fourth grade.

But something caught Mohandas's eye when he was told this, and his gaze wandered. Maybe he noticed something far off in the sky. The wrinkles tensed on his face and the sparkle vanished from his eyes. A gruff voice emerged as if out of some deep cavern: 'I finished my BA, with honours. Studied day and night. Look where it got me.'

And then the twinkle would return, and his cracked lips broke into a smile. 'I'm learning computers now. I go to the Star Computer Centre near the bus stand. Shakil owns the computer centre, he's the son of Mohammad Imran who runs the building supply and hardware store, and he told me, "If you can learn how to type well, do layout and printing, I'll pay you more than six hundred a month."' Mohandas continued, 'This month I'm up to thirty words per minute. I'm working a few small typing jobs, but the thing is that it takes a lot of time to correct the mistakes, and I make a lot of them.'

But this was old news. A serious calamity had now befallen Mohandas, who kept repeating:

'My name isn't Mohandas. I'm ready to go to court and sign an affidavit. Whoever wants to be Mohandas, let him be Mohandas. Please, do whatever you can to help! I beg all of you!'

What sort of dire straits was Mohandas in?

But before getting into that, I'd first like to finish describing the fifth member of Mohandas's family, his six-year-old daughter, Sharda. Six-year-old Sharda goes to school in the government primary school in the village, and is a student in the second grade. After school, she sets off for Bichhiya Tola, another village that's two-and-a-half kilometres away, crossing two ponds on the way. She doesn't get back home before half past nine or ten at night. In Bichhiya Tola she looks after the one-year-old son of Bisnath Prasad, and does household chores like sweeping and cleaning. In exchange for her services, she's fed supper and given thirty rupees a month.

Nagendranath was one of the major farmers of Bichhiya village. He was also a manager in the life insurance company; his connections reached everyone from the district collector to the local MP. He'd been head of the local panchayat twice and the district director once. Bisnath Prasad, whose one-year-old was looked after by Sharada, was one of the sons of Nagendranath, one of the village elders. Even though his real name was Vishwanath Prasad, everyone in the village called him Bisnath, and said behind his back, 'He's a real viper, a first-rate poison pusher. One squirt from his mouth and the show's over! The father's Cobranath and the son's Vipernath. If he spies you and starts to smile, words dripping with honey – better watch out! That means he's ready to strike.' Of all the things Bisnath possessed, honour was not among them. Sometimes he'd get drunk and say, 'Pull the wool over someone's eyes? That's fun, but what's more fun is pulling down the skirt of your wife and finding her wool, ha!' No gentle words were ever spoken about the people he consorted with, either from within the village, or without.

Bisnath was from a high caste, Mohandas a low Kabirpanthi weaver. Many of Mohandas's brethren still wove mats and rugs and blankets. Mohandas wasn't merely the first member of his

49

community from the village to get a college degree, but the first in the entire region. And he not only finished his degree, but also graduated second in his class.

(Please stop for a moment and tell the truth: did you begin to get the feeling that I'd gone and started telling you some kind of encoded, symbol-laden tale? The main character of the story is called Mohandas, the wife is Kasturibai, the mother is Putlibai and the son's name is Devdas…?

Kasturibai reminds you of Kasturba – and, well, Mohandas couldn't be more clear. If you read Mahatma Gandhi's auto-biography, also known as *The Story of My Experiments with Truth*, you'll discover that his father, Karamchand, was also called Kaba. And His mother was Putlibai… and who doesn't know the tale of his son, Devdas? Look at Mohandas, his build, and the state he's in: he shares the same history as the Mahatma. The difference is that Mohandas looks the way he does not because of Porbandar – the place where Gandhi was born – or Kathiawar, Rajkot, England, South Africa, or Birla House, but as a result of the hunger and heat, sweat and sickness, insult and injustice in the fields and pastures, caverns and caves, jungles and marshes, of Chhattisgarh and Vindhya Pradesh. Otherwise, all the rest is the same.

I'd also like to stop the story right here and now to solemnly affirm that the similarity of names is honestly and truly just a coincidence. When I sat down to write this, I had no idea these sorts of echoes could possibly be hidden in the story of Mohandas and his family from the village.

You'll have to take my word, and don't read too much into it. It isn't some symbolic story or allegory or coded fable. It's totally on the level. Though, truth be told, it's not really a story.

As I'm wont to do, I wind up detailing the real life of a real person – someone alive now, living among us in our society – concealing it behind the veil of a story. Mohandas is a living, breathing human being, and his life is at this moment in grave danger. Though you can count on my having played a little fast and loose with the truth, as I always do.

My game, however, is like the game of trying to hide an elephant with a washcloth.

Assume that the elephant is a truth. If a poet or writer tries to hide the animal behind a meagre washcloth, he risks burning his bridges and sinking the boats that ferry him through the journey of life.

Mohandas is real. If you'd like to verify this, you can do so by asking any inhabitant of our village, or any other village in this country.)

Mohandas's mother and father had high hopes that when he got his BA he would soon find a good job. He'd been married by the age of fifteen to Kasturi, the daughter of Biranju, from Katkona village. She was a hard worker. After arriving at her in-laws' after the wedding, she immediately began looking after the entire household, even taking on small chores for the neighbours; the money she earned allowed Mohandas to pay his college fees. Everyone was watching Mohandas, the first young man from his caste to get a college degree, and at the top of the class. When the exam results were announced, his photo was published in the local papers. Test prep companies even used his photo in their publicity materials.

Mohandas duly registered with the job office, and sent off application after application for openings he'd found in the classifieds. Time and again he received postcards from the job office. He then studied for the public service exam, working much harder than he'd ever worked as a student.

Mohandas travelled anywhere and everywhere looking for work. Though he'd aced his exams at college, he was never invited back after the job interviews. And then he'd discover the people getting hired were those with barely a high school education, if that, or the ones who had graduated in the middle or bottom of their classes. All of them had some kind of connection: either they were the son-in-law, or son, or nephew, or brown noser, or assistant, to a government officer, politician, or big shot. Mohandas came home after every interview with the feeling his luck was running out, but he didn't give up hope. He knew full well how corrupt India was – but what about the ten or twenty per cent who found work on the basis on merit and hard work?

He realised after a while that some of the positions were auctioned off to the highest bidder. If his father had had fifty or a hundred thousand rupees, Mohandas could have used that as a bribe to get two or three jobs that had otherwise slipped away.

Time went on. He was now past the age limit for a government position. His family began to lose hope. Still, Kasturi kept up her encouragement: *No government work, no problem, you'll get something in the private sector. Or else pick up a trade. The government has plenty of opportunities nowadays for the out-of-work educated. We'll raise chickens. We'll start a brisk business selling eggs. We'll open a shop to make candles or incense, or a little flourmill. Government banks are giving out loans.* One time a literacy job came up; he could have found temporary work as a teacher. But in the end it turned out the government official who was in charge of the program was only hiring people from his own caste or political party;

Mohandas was of a different caste, and didn't belong to any political party.

He was totally straightforward; a bit reserved, and had plenty of self-respect. And, sadly, it simply wasn't in his power to do as much running around as he would have been required to, kissing the arses of government officers or hakims, bribing them with food and drink. And like the jobs themselves, looking for a job was a bloodsport, full of rivalry. It's not as if Mohandas was afraid of competition – if he had been, how would he have graduated with honours? But he soon discovered the real world was one massive sports stadium, and the ones who scored goal after goal were those who had the power to cripple the other players. And this power came from criminal, illegal connections and back-door deals, nepotism and nefariousness, bribes and rewards – none of which Mohandas had access to.

It wasn't just Mohandas, but his whole family that began to let go of the dream of his becoming a government officer or hakim, and with great difficulty began to hope that he would just find some job, any job that would free him from joblessness and emptiness, and at least bring home some money to feed the family. This is when his father, Kaba, was diagnosed with TB. He began wheezing, and coughing up blood. And just a little while later Putlibai's eyes were ruined by the free eye clinic. On top of all of the housework and small jobs she did to earn money, now Kasturi had become the caretaker for her in-laws. This was also when she was in most need of rest, since she was pregnant – Devdas had arrived in her womb.

Looking at Mohandas, you'd think he'd been sick for a long time. He didn't visit many people from the village. It also became more and more difficult for him to face his fellow villagers or caste brethren, so he avoided them all. The same question was on everyone's lips: 'What's he up to, and has he sorted out a job yet?

The Kathina river flowed nearby. Like most people from the village, Mohandas planted various melons, cucumbers, and gourds in the summer months on its banks. His wife and parents joined him – they dug irrigation ditches to bring water to the seedlings. They worked in shifts, afternoons and evenings, watching over everything to make sure the digging went smoothly; the crops brought them an extra nine or ten thousand rupees per year. Though a few times the monsoon came at the wrong time, causing the river level to rise; whatever crops had been ready for harvest were washed away by the swelling current. Twice this happened to Mohandas. A dark pessimism began to grow inside.

Mohandas hadn't come home the night Kasturi gave birth to Devdas. He'd been lying on the wide sandy bank of the Kathina, keeping an eye on the quiet sky above. It happened to be a new moon the night Devdas was born. Kasturi almost didn't live through the delivery; the umbilical cord got twisted around the infant's neck, with little Devdas stuck halfway out. Bilspurhin, who'd come to help with the delivery, announced that Kasturi, who'd passed out from fear, was in mortal danger.

Mohandas's blind mother and coughing father looked everywhere to find their son, but he was nowhere to be found. He was lying on the sandy bank of the Kathina, staring up at the moonless sky like a corpse, searching for some sign of life inside him. The dark black of the new moon night, not blood, flowed through his veins. His gloomy mind couldn't find sleep, it swarmed with visions of terror that had incubated in the womb of a system thoroughly rotten and corrupt.

Mohandas had probably passed out on the banks of the river that night – otherwise, he would have heard his mother and father calling him, or his wife shrieking, or his newborn son Devdas crying when he was born at four in the morning.

The sun had already risen well into the sky by the time its rays awakened Mohandas, who was lying on the banks of the Kathina one kilometre outside the village, out of his sleep, or swoon.

Mohandas lay still in the sand for a long time as he warmed up. His body was spent, his thoughts scattered. It began to dawn on him that he wasn't on his balcony or in his courtyard; he was sprawled on the sandy riverbank, where he'd planted cucumbers and melons and loki and tomatoes just a few days ago. But the rains had come too soon, and the river had first swelled, then overflowed, until its ravenous crest had swallowed everything whole.

Mohandas returned home to find quite a crowd from the village assembled; women, too. It seemed they were all talking about him, and the crowd hushed and people scattered as soon as he arrived.

'It was by the grace of god she pulled through, son. The villagers had already come with the tulsi leaf and said she was nearly dead,' his mother said, wiping the tears away with a corner of her sari. 'I swear that baby's some kind of angel.'

He went into his wife's little chamber. Kasturi was lying on the cot, sleeping with her baby; moments earlier, she'd been on the brink of death. Smoke from the cow dung cake burning in the borsi pot filled the room, along with the smell of the neem water and musty ajwain. Her eyes barely registered Mohandas's presence; his heart sank when he saw how exhausted she was, how vulnerable. One more stomach had delivered itself to the house that morning. Arrangements for half a litre of cow's milk would have to be made daily for nine months. Kasturi would need a diet of turmeric rice, ginger, ghee, and sweet gur for a month. And then he'd have to spend all kinds of money feeding relatives for the birth ceremony, the naming ceremony, the annaprashan milk-and-rice newborn feeding ceremony. And then... his gaze fell on the newborn sleeping against his mother's side, a hale and hearty, pudgy little fellow, beautiful and innocent, snuggled against her, looking like the offspring of some divine being. Mohandas felt fatherly feelings well up inside for the first time, and he simply couldn't take his eyes off of the boy.

'The postman Sitaram's here and he's got something for you,' Kaba called from the balcony.

Mohandas read the letter, from the biggest coal mine in the district, inviting Mohandas for an interview. It'd been more than a few months since he'd received this kind of invitation. Was it possible that while he lay in the sand on the banks of the Kathina his thoughts had produced some kind of sound that reached high up in the sky, finally reaching a celestial body? That a heavenly being perceived his sorrow, his calamitous state? Was the baby Kasturi gave birth to in the wee hours of the morning an angel who would unlock the door to a whole new life for his entire family?

The interview letter sent to by Oriental Coal Mines via the employment agency glowed with the promise of a new beginning. After a long drought, a tender sprout of hope grew once again in Mohandas's heart. He couldn't sleep the next night; though he had accepted the fact that his tree of life had been reduced to a dead stump, now it exploded with new shoots.

On the day of his interview, Mohandas arrived one hour early. Invoking the names of his family goddess, Malihamai, and his spiritual guru, Kabirdas, he experienced an unprecedented feeling of self-confidence, hungry for the job no matter what. A one hour written exam would be followed by an hour's break, followed by the physical test. He dived into the tasks with all his mind and soul. He finished the hour-long exam in less than thirty minutes. The questions were easy, and multiple-choice; he had only to write a check mark next to the correct answer. For the two-hour physical exam they made him run a 1500-metre dash, then a sprint, then lift some weights, then crawl on all fours over rough terrain, and finally run five laps around the field. He took an eye exam; they had him identify various colours. He didn't come in second in any of these performances.

At four in the afternoon, the door opened to the office where the hundred and fifty other job applicants were sitting. The names of the five candidates that had been selected were called out, and Mohandas's was number one.

His heart beat wildly – the impossible was happening. A quick end to all his life's uncertainties. Every month, a pay cheque. Every day, a fire in the stove at home, and a hot, steaming curry. Medical treatment for his mother and father. No more need for Kasturi to work like a dog in the homes of others.

The clerk had assembled all of Mohandas's diplomas and transcripts. Looking over his BA transcript he said, 'Huh? You haven't found a job yet? With just a little shoulder to the grind-stone and you should've been able to find something decent.'

'How soon can I start?' Mohandas asked.

'Consider yourself started. We'll have all your papers pro-cessed by the end of the week at the latest, and then the contract will be sent to your house. At most the whole process will take two weeks.'

It was the dawn of a new era at the home of Mohandas. He had two thousand rupees sitting at the post office, and with it he bought a new mosquito net, a kilo of ghee, sweet gur, dried ginger, a few good pots and pans, new clothes for Kasturi and Devdas. For himself he bought a pair of jeans, a poly blend shirt with a checked pattern, a thirty-rupee wallet, a couple of five-rupee handkerchiefs. He made arrangements with Parasu for a half litre of milk to be delivered each morning. Word spread in the village that, at long last, Mohandas had found an honest-to-goodness job. Villagers who had utterly shunned Mohandas began to be civil, even solicitous. People who'd made fun of his degree and hard work began to sing a different tune.

'It was just a matter of time. Mohandas couldn't have sat around empty-handed for very long with his kind of degree.'

And then there were others who made comments like this: 'You know that bamboo-weaver-whatever caste Mohandas belongs to? They've got job quotas for them now too. And he's the one who got the quota job for his caste since he was the only one of the lot there with a degree.'

And kheer, too, was served for dessert at Mohandas's home that week, and a delicious potato-tomato curry – and spicy! His mother forgot about her blindness as her fingers felt and groped around the little winnowing basket to pick out the pebbles from the rice and dhal. She even used mustard oil to make a chicken dish with red chili and dried mango powder. Kaba bought a full pack of Mangalore Ganesh bidis and a box of Nai Jahaz-brand matches – a gentle strike, and they lit up like a torch. He sat out on the balcony for many nights, taking long, satisfying puffs on his bidi, singing bhajans in praise of Kabirdas at the top of his lungs. And he didn't cough once, and there wasn't any blood in his phlegm.

One morning at the crack of dawn blind Putlibai was nearly pirouetting in the courtyard, singing with all the joy in her heart:

> My boy, his wife, they've come to settle down
> And so has the little bird myna, in the same room, she's
>   nested 'round
> Call it a holy sign, call it a holy sign, and our troubles
>   will wash away
> Jai ho to Goddess Maliha! Success and victory and more
> Jai ho to Satguru Maharaj! Victory and success to you

The next week Mohandas waited every day for the letter to arrive from the coal mine. But the postman didn't come. And then the next week, too – no letter. It was going on three weeks, and by then he'd heard that Santosh Kumar Sharma, son of Kanchan Mal Sharma from Kansakora, was the first to receive his papers. Mohandas caught the state bus service to the coal mine, and was told by the same clerk in the recruitment office that the letters were in the process of being sent out. There were, in fact, only three positions for the five men picked; if no more spots opened up, they'd have to strike two candidates from the list. Mohandas was terrified; the clerk saw the disappointment on his face and tried to reassure him by saying that he hoped that two more positions would open up and even if they didn't Mohandas's name still wouldn't be struck from the list since his had been at the very top.

Mohandas went home. The clerk had told him to wait another six weeks, and had tried to sound as convincing as possible, but Mohandas had already lost a little of his verve. He thought about how Parsu would want his money at the end of the month for the daily milk. In all the excitement, he'd borrowed more money; how was he going to pay it back now? Kasturi told him to keep his resolve. Putlibai promised goddess Maliha whatever she wanted if she saw Mohandas through. And, well, Kaba didn't say very much; the singing stopped and the cough came back.

Six weeks later Mohandas returned to the Oriental Coal Mines. He waited for a long time before the clerk called him into the recruitment office, where again he told him to wait a little longer. This time he didn't say for how long, and the bonhomie had faded from his demeanor. Before leaving, Mohandas emphasised that he'd be back again in a month to see if there was anything new; indifferently, the clerk replied, 'Why bother? If you get the letter, you get the letter.' Then he added, 'The truth is that the Coal India manager who chose the candidates that day was from Bihar and gave one of the jobs to his son-in-law. These are the kinds of games the higher-ups play.' A dark pit opened before Mohandas.

The next month Mohandas went again to see if he could find something out – you never know. He was made to wait outside the office from half past ten in the morning until half past three in the afternoon. After pleading and cajoling with the underling, Mohandas was allowed inside the office, only to discover that the other clerk was on vacation, and that the fat clerk filling in for him knew nothing about his file. Mohandas expressed his concern about the whereabouts of his college transcript and other original documents; by way of an answer, the fat clerk asked what in the world they would do with his transcript and certificates, and added that if Mohandas didn't get the job, the office would return them by registered mail. Otherwise he could come and pick them up himself the next time he came.

Again Mohandas went home. He knew in his heart of hearts that the gods in the skies had truly sensed his disaster, and had therefore showered drops of mercy onto the dead stump of his existence; the ugly burl had wondrously sprouted shoots and buds, about to burst wide open. But the backdraft of corruption and bad luck had burned it all away. Now no hope remained. If he'd had some cash on hand he could have found a middleman to take it to the top, and secure him the position. The rich in the village were the first to get wind of Mohandas's situation; just as they'd done before, they started making fun of his education and skills. Mohandas had to swallow the bitter pill of humiliation the day he ran into Vijay Tiwari, son of Pandit Chatradhari, with whom he'd studied at college; and who, even though barely managing to graduate – at the bottom of the class at that – had been set up with a job as a police sub-inspector, thanks to his in-laws' behind-the-scenes deals. He summoned Mohandas.

'Moe-huh-naaa! Mo-ha-na! Just the other day I bought three water buffalo as part of a government sponsored program. You see, I'm going to start a dairy. If you play your cards right, you and dear Kasturi can tend to the buffalo, feed them, look after them. You'll get paid on the first of the month, and I'll get your house fixed up through the Indira Awas program. And that sweetheart Kasturi shall have a good time in our milk dairy!'

'Let me think it over,' Mohandas replied, concealing the insult oozing inside. Hearing the name of Kasturi emerge from Vijay Tiwari's mouth deepened his feelings of impotence, and gave rise to a new, formless fear. If something weren't done, and fast, his family would break open and shatter into a thousand pieces. He had to come up with something, anything that was within his power, and something that didn't require anyone else's help or connections. Swirling around him were images of Kasturi's lovely face and Vijay Tiwari's cunning stare.

He decided then and there that he wouldn't go back to the Oriental Coal Mines to find out what happened to his diploma, transcript, and the rest of his certificates. Why should he? They weren't even worth the paper they were printed on. He and people like him didn't have whatever it was that it took to secure jobs, or to get their hands in the cookie jar of government project funds.

After dinner that night, Mohandas didn't sleep. He gathered seedlings and a spade, slung everything over his shoulder, told Kasturi he'd be back in the morning, and set off for the banks of the Kathina, and, once there, worked like a spirit possessed to dig irrigation channels for the seedlings of muskmelon, cucumber, watermelon, tomato, and eggplant. At around four thirty in the morning, when all the other stars, one after another, began to fade, but the North Star was still shining with all its lustre, Mohandas wiped the sweat from his forehead and chest and slowly began wading into the waters of the Kathina. Dipping his cupped hands in the water, he scooped the water back over his head, placed his flat palms together in supplication, and said with great emotion, 'Just please don't wash away the little plants, Kathinamai. Have mercy on Malihamai, have mercy on my son Devdas. Please don't gobble up all the crops I planted from the sweat of my brow! Because if you do I'll jump right in, height of the monsoon, with my kids and all, and fill your stomach with us!'

Tears from his eyes dripped down from his face to swim in the Kathina, where tiny kothari fish swam to the surface and fought to nip at the salt from his teardrops, while Mohandas emerged from the river with Kabirdas's name on his lips.

When Mohandas got home he found Kasturi busy plastering the courtyard with cowdung, Putlibai sorting by touch the seeds of the muskmelon, cucumber, watermelon in her winnowing basket, Kaba, who had found some shade in the corner, engrossed in husking the bamboo, and eighteen-month-old baby Devdas in his own little world sitting in the middle of the courtyard playing an innocent game of chopping grass with a little cutting tool.

Hearing the sound of his footsteps, Putlibai looked up with her sightless eyes and met Mohandas's with a smile. 'Did you hear, Mohana, that mama myna gave birth to two chicks in the myna nest?'

If she'd been able to see she would have been happy to note the look of joy that shone on Mohandas's face when he heard the news.

After supper that night Mohandas took Devdas and Kasturi with him down to the Kathina. Kasturi had collected all the seeds and kept them safe in the folds of the sari at her waist, and had hoisted Devdas firmly on her shoulders. Long-grass rope, a spade, and trowel were slung over Mohandas's shoulders.

A few little breaths of the cool river air, and it wasn't long before Devdas was off in a deep sleeping reverie. Kasturi and Mohandas got to work filling the seedling holes he'd dug with the cow dung fertiliser and planting the various seedlings for the fruits and vegetables. It took two hours before the work was completed. Kasturi brought water from the Kathina in a ghari pot and sprinkled it over the seedbeds; Mohandas was transfixed by her beauty under the twinkling starlight. In the waning moonlight, Kasturi's dusky body looked just like the old stone statues that lay outside the little temple of Malihamai, the ones brought after their excavation from Benheru talab. Kasturi matched those beautiful bodies – her waist, arms, breasts, legs – as if a sculptor had spent years doing nothing but carefully chiselling her form.

It was well past midnight; they could hear the occasional sandpiper or pankukri. All Mohandas could smell was the scent of the sweat on Kasturi's body, mixed with the heaviness of the river air. What sort of dreams did she have when she married him – and then how did things turn out? From morning 'til night, day in and day out, without fail, good times or bad, healthy or sick, whether food was on the table or not, she was there, standing beside Mohandas. He felt a deep bond with her, utterly intimate, and he couldn't stop staring. She placed the clay jar down on the sand, stood up, and began braiding her hair. Mohandas approached; she was silent.

'Fancy a game of kabaddi?' Mohandas suggested with a little smile. 'Hu, Tu, Tu, it's like wrestling!'

He grabbed hold of her arm, and began tickling her stomach and armpits. She tried to squirm away, 'Arré, arré, you'll wake up Devdas, what are you doing? Pleasestop pleasestop pleasestop!'

When she realised Mohandas wasn't about to let go, she gave him a little push, broke free and ran toward the river. She leapt like a mad doe, suddenly free, running beneath the hazy, dimming light of the celestial bodies in the sky that shone on the sandy bank that stretched off as far as the eye could see.

'C'mon and catch me if you c-a-a-a-a-n-n-n! And if you do, I'll know you *can* and *more*,' she teased, her voice trailing off as she ran far into the distance, her shadow vanishing.

'Hu, tu, tu, I'm coming after you!' Mohandas said as he set off at a sprint toward her.

Kasturi quickened her pace, but Mohandas was catching up. As she ran faster, giving it all she had, her feet splashed water on the riverbanks. 'C'mon and catch me if you c-a-a-a-a-n-n-n!' She was getting winded. Mohandas's 'Hu, tu, tu, I'm coming after you!' grew closer with every second. She realised she wasn't going to be able to get away, but nonetheless gave it one more go – and just as she was picking up speed, Mohandas managed to catch up with one great leap and grab hold of her; they plunged into the waters. 'Lemmego! Lemmego!' she said trying to fend him off, splashing him with water, but Mohandas just held on tighter. His breath and her breath commingled in the wet river air. He tickled her as before, this time yielding great laughter. She dropped her false resistance, and in the middle of pushing him away, her body slid up right to his, like iron to a magnet.

He flipped her down onto the shallow riverbed and slid atop her. 'My sweet little beauty!' And he began to kiss her. They flopped and splashed, unbound in the cool waters of the Kathina, as if they were two young fish, maybe a gonch or padhit, frolicking under the hazy, flickering stars in that hot monsoon midnight. Occasionally a sweet scream of delight emerged from deep in Kasturi's bosom, piercing the night's stillness, and mixed with Mohandas's heavily breathed 'Hu, tu, tu tuuuuu!'

An exhausted Kasturi emerged from the water and fell asleep in her soaking wet sari, Devdas at her side. As for Mohandas, he remained lying in the shallow waters of the Kathina river for who knows how many hours, eyes fixed on the gods in the sky, and singing:

> Birds are singing, *chirp chirp*!
> *Chirp chirp* but where is my sweet lover?
> My lover in this cherry blossom season?
> Wild cherry where have you gone?
> How to tell my cherry I am ready but not yet ripe?

Mohandas had such a sweet singing voice that night that the lapwings and pankukris in the far-away distance heard his song and joined in.

That night would later be remembered as the beginning of Sharda.

It was a good year for muskmelon and watermelon and vegetables in general, but the price remained low at the market, and there wasn't any real profit to be had. Again Kasturi was pregnant and had to take on more work, while Mohandas toiled like an animal. While that one time the Kathina had heeded his prayers, afterward its waters often crested high, its current gobbling up a month's worth of Mohandas's labor. Kaba's cough began to worsen, but Mohandas met an excellent doctor, Dr Wakankar, who worked six miles away at the government hospital in the neighbouring village, and explained that TB drugs were available free in the hospital, and that his father

66

should get the full course of medicine. The doctor gave him a plastic bag with a full two months' worth of the drug. But Kaba wasn't capable by himself of taking the medications on time, and he didn't take his meals or eat according to any sort of normal schedule. Dr Wakankar also told Mohandas that his mother could have an operation done that would restore some of her eyesight, but it would run to at least ten thousand. He gave his word to Mohandas that if ever an honest district collector came to the area, he'd arrange the operation; but years passed without an honest district collector coming to the area. In the meantime, a young man and woman from an NGO started visiting their weaver-caste neighbourhood, and made all sorts of promises about some project that would greatly increase their quality of life. The two youths filled out a bunch of forms, and had Mohandas sign them. But then the visits stopped; later they found out that the two had got married and gone to Delhi. She was working for a TV channel and, thanks to an uncle of his, he'd been set up with a cushy IAS job in a slum development, and was now opening his own foundation, taking trips criss-crossing India and the globe.

Time marched on with Mohandas and Kasturi somehow managing to survive by the grace of Malihamai and their own hard work. Sharda was two, Devdas four. Kaba now spent most of his time stretched out on the cot. Sometimes he'd help make some long-grass rope or husk the bamboo. But his cough got worse and worse, and he was so skinny you could count his ribs. Sometimes it seemed as if he were spewing chunks of his own flesh mixed with the blood. And meanwhile some bigwigs had found a way to have Dr Wakankar transferred to some other district, leaving no one in the hospital who would provide the

TB drugs free of charge. Whenever Mohandas went to inquire, he was told to come back next week. Kaba had weakened to the extent that he just lay on the cot staring silently at the ground after each fit of coughing. Insects began to recognise the sound of his hack. Yellow and black ants set off in droves the moment his spit hit the spot next to his bed where he spat. A swarm of horseflies attacked the moment he coughed, nearly giving Kaba a heart attack, and it looked like the end was near. He tried calling out for Putlibai, but was seized in a coughing fit before he could get the words out; finally, he ended up filling his cupped hands with a mass of spit and blood and tissue. Mohandas and Kasturi had been gone for a while looking after the plantings at the river's edge, and blind Putlibai was the only one at home. She went tripping and scrambling to Kaba's side, began touching her husband's body all over, crying. Rheumatism had stiffened her joints over the past year. Kaba lay absolutely still. After a little while after his breathing steadied he began to chastise Putlibai.

'Hey blindy, why all the tears? I'm not about to kick the bucket yet. First I am going to attend Devdas's wedding, then send Sharda off to her new husband. After that, I can die. Stop crying!'

He touched his hand to his wife's head.

'Bring me the whittler and some bamboo.'

(Let's stop here for a minute. I bet you're thinking that I'm taking advantage of the one hundred and twenty fifth anniversary of the birth of Premchand, the King of Hindi Fiction, to spin you some hundred-and-twenty-five-year-old story dressed up as a tale of today. But the truth is that the account I am putting before you, in its old and backward style, manner, and language, is a tale of a time right after 9/11, in the aftermath of the collapse of the World Trade Center in New York; a time when two sovereign Asian nations were reduced to ash and rubble. It's a tale of a time when anybody worshipping any gods other than the god of the US and Europe were called fascists, terrorists, religious fanatics. Gas and oil, water, markets, profit, plunder: to get all of this, companies, governments, and armies were killing innocent people every day all over the world.

A time when, if you looked closely, you'd notice that everyone in power was a clone of one another, when everyone was consuming the same brands, drinking the same drinks, eating the same foods, driving the same cars made by the same car companies, bank account in the same kinds of banks. Everyone had the same kind of ATM card in their pocket and same mobile phone in their hands. They got drunk on the same booze, and you could see them on page three of the newspaper on any of the TV channels from 1 to 70, soused, naked, outrageous. Look closely and you'll notice they all have the same skin tone and speak the same language.)

The colour was totally washed out of Mohandas's blue jeans and checked shirt, and both were covered with patches Kasturi had sewn on. Kaba left his bed only if he had to answer the call of nature, but otherwise slept day and night, coughing and spitting up phlegm. Putlibai groaned incessantly from the pain of her rheumatism. And yet when they were in the presence of their grandchildren, Devdas and Sharda, the rickety frames of grand-mother and grandfather overflowed with life and tenderness and devotion to the little ones. Devdas jumped up and down on his baba Kaba's cot while little Sharda stubbornly stuck to her aaji Putlibai's lap and horsed around.

That day Mohandas and Kasturi were busy weaving bamboo mats, bamboo pith helmets, and little purses woven from bamboo. They'd received such an enormous order from Vindhyachal Handicrafts – Mohanlal Marwari's shop – that for the past ten or twelve weeks they'd done nothing but try to finish it. Kaba and Putli looked after the children. The order was for fifty mats, fifty hats, and thirty purses. Kaba got up from his cot when his cough wasn't rendering him immobile and helped husk the bamboo; it was an ancient craft, and he had a lot of experience. Kasturi wove the mats as if her fingers were working a machine. Four-and-a-half year old Devdas had put a hat over his head and with a bamboo stick in hand was driving two-year-old Sharda as if she were a goat, shouting, 'hurry up, get along!'; wee Sharda in turn crawled on all fours as best she could from one corner of the room to the other. Just then there was a knock on the door. It was Kasturi's brother-in-law, Gopaldas, who, leaning his bike against the wall, came inside. He worked as a saw operator at Narmada Timber and Furniture at the bazaar, and the owner also sent him on errands to collect various small debts.

Kasturi was delighted to see Gopaldas. It had been a long time since a visitor had come from a village near her home. After offering him something to drink and sharing a smoke, Gopal told Mohandas that he'd been at the Oriental Coal Mines three days ago on business. While there, he found out that Bisnath from Bichiya Tola had been working there under the name of Mohandas for the past five years as deputy depot supervisor, earning more than ten thousand a month. Gopaldas also found out that Bisnath's father Nagendranath had gone to the clerk in the recruitment office and wrangled Mohandas's employment letter out of him, then given it to his wayward son. Bisnath took advantage of the fact that the transcripts and diploma Mohandas had brought at the time of his interview didn't have his photos on them, so he presented himself as Mohandas, and put his own photos where Mohandas's photos would have been, then went to court and had all the documents notarised by the gazetted officer. Bisnath had transformed himself into Mohandas, son of Kabadas, caste Kabirpanthi Vishwakarma, and was taking home ten thousand a month as deputy depot supervisor, a position he filled with great confidence.

Gopaldas had seen Bisnath near the mine at a food stall drinking chai. He saw the plastic ID card hanging around his neck: it was Mohandas's name, but Bisnath's photo. And on top of that, everyone drinking chai with him was calling him 'Mohandas.'

What's more, Bisnath had left his home in Bichiya Tola village four years ago and had moved with his entire family to the workers quarters, called Lenin Nagar, where his wife made more than a few rupees with her own small time loan sharking; she also ran a shady chit fund. It was bizarre how all Bisnath's fellow workers called him 'Mohandas' and his wife Amita 'Kasturi Madam.' Bisnath had not, like Mohandas, earned a BA, but rather was a tenth-grade drop-out; so rather than doing any work in the mine, he spent his time arse-kissing managers, skimming whatever coal he could, and busying himself with union politics.

71

Mohandas's mind was spinning as he heard what his brother-in-law was telling him. How could this happen? Even if the world's turned upside-down, how can one man become another? And like this, out in the open, in broad daylight? And not just for the afternoon, temporarily, but for four whole years? And yet, in his poverty and powerlessness, Mohandas – given the days that he'd seen and the old stories he'd heard from Kaba about his own life – began to feel as if the officers and the hakims and the wealthy and the party members were so powerful, they could turn anything into anything: a dog into an ox, a pig into a lion, a ditch into a mountain, a thief into a gentleman. Mohandas could hardly catch his breath. O guru, what kind of time are we living in when not one person in four long years has been able to step forward and say that the man working at the Oriental Coal Mines who calls himself Mohandas and earns ten thousand a month isn't Mohandas, but Bisnath; that his father isn't Kaba, he's Nagendranath, his wife isn't Kasturi, it's Amita Bhardwaj, his mother isn't Putlibai, but Renukadevi, who isn't from Purbanra village, but lives in Bichiya Tola? Who doesn't have a BA, but who dropped out of tenth grade?

Mohandas lost focus that day and kept stopping weaving the mats. His gaze wandered off and he became lost in thought. His hands slipped as he wove the bamboo, and he nearly cut his thumb with the sickle. Katuri kept an eye on him the whole time, knowing exactly the kind of roiling was going on inside. She took the knife from his hand and said, 'The sun's a bit much today, why don't you wash up and have a rest?'

The next morning Mohandas caught the seven o'clock bus and set off for the Oriental Coal Mines. The night before he couldn't sleep. The bus arrived at the mine at half past ten.

72

Who could he go talk to? That was the first problem. He didn't know anyone. On top of that, the way he looked would make it hard for people to believe that he was the real Mohandas who'd graduated with a BA at the top of his class at M. G. College, and whose photo just a few years ago was in the newspaper. Another problem was that he didn't have any copies of the newspaper, and therefore wouldn't be able to point to the photo and say, 'Look, that's me, Mohandas, son of Kabadas, resident of Purbanra, district Annuppur, Madhya Pradesh, the one who a few years ago got his BA at M. G. Degree College, the one who graduated at the top of his class and was number two in merit. See the resemblance? It's me, Mohandas!'

It wasn't easy, but Mohandas managed to sneak in through the gate and into the company compound. His jeans were torn at the knee, and were beginning to rip at the back, too, but Kasturi had patched those bits up with matching colours she'd used from scraps of fabric from a sari top or bedcover. Exposure to the elements and heat and cold and hunger and hard work had turned his skin a dark copper. Sorrow and calamity had scored his face with so many wrinkles that no one would ever believe he was younger than forty. Enduring want and quietly eating insult and injury had made the hair on his head and all over his body a little greyer. Mohandas was in his early thirties but looked as if he was in his fifties.

Mohandas stood in front of the same office where, four years ago, he'd brought his diploma and certificates, and where the employment clerk assured him that his name could never be crossed off the list since he'd had the highest marks for both the written and physical exams.

And sitting in the very same office was the very same clerk. He had a bigger chair now and a bigger desk in front of him to match; the air conditioner behind his desk provided him with a constant cool breeze. Mohandas stood in the doorway watching him busily eating tea biscuits and drinking chai, while two people sat in front of his desk chatting with him, as if they had all the time in the world.

At once the clerk noticed Mohandas, who quickly pressed his hands into a *namaskar*, and smiled a big smile with the hope that it'd jog the clerk's memory. But the clerk looked put out – maybe he didn't recognise Mohandas? He tried again, joined his hands again into a *namaste* and said brightly, 'Sir, it's Mohandas...!' But by then the clerk had pressed the button beneath his desk that rang the bell. It had a hard clanging ring, and the underling appeared immediately. Mohandas couldn't make out exactly what the clerk said to him, but they were clearly words of scolding. He emerged from the room, drew the curtain, and looked Mohandas over from head to toe with a scowl. 'What business do you have here? Go sit on the bench outside. How the devil did you get in here?' Mohandas wanted to tell the clerk that his name was Mohandas, and that four years ago he'd been offered a job here at the coal mine, and that all of his papers were sitting in that office, but then what happened was that some other man stole his name and stole the job... But Mohandas's voice was too feeble, and the underling manhandled him over to the bench, and his utterances made no sense. There was a lump in his throat and he was stammering. Breaking free with one of his arms from the underling's grip he managed to spit out, '*Dada*, I need to see that clerk, just for a minute to pick up my papers and transcript.'

The underling more or less pushed him over onto the wooden bench that sat against the wall, turned around, and went back. Mohandas knew that he'd never be allowed back in; this was his last chance. He called after the man, who was just about to disappear inside the employment office.

'Hey! HEY! Go tell that clerk that Mohandas, BA, is here, and he wants all the papers and certificates back he deposited here on 18 August 1997. What a bungle! Give you a nice room and big chair and then it's nothing but anarchy? Grab a piece of paper, take down my name. Then go show it to your boss!'

The underling's jaw dropped. Here was a guy dressed in rags who looked like a hobo, yet the language that came out of his mouth was quite lucid, even eloquent, and his manner equal to a educated manager, or clerk's.

The man remained planted in the doorway and just stared at Mohandas: his washed-out, patched-up jeans; his mended, dirty checked shirt; his balding head, hair that'd turned half-grey; his lustreless, burnt-copper face, criss-crossed with crooked wrinkles; deep-set eyes, gloomy and weak, as if they were seeing a reflection of themselves; his cheap sandals stuck to his feet, their ancient rubber molested by penury and despair, now turned into dirt and wood and paper.

'You son-of-a-bitch!' the angry underling muttered under his breath. 'You crazy bastard! Hey motherfucker, you think the big man will help your beggar butt?'

Mohandas surmised that the underling didn't really believe what he was saying, even though god himself knew it was all true, so he stood up from the bench and walked toward the man with sure steps, maybe even with a little swagger. He had in mind that he would go in and try to explain that it wasn't just that Bisnath had taken him for a ride, but had played the entire Oriental Coal Mines for a fool.

The way Mohandas was striding toward him, the impatience and swiftness, the taut wrinkles on his face that mirrored the distress in his mind, his deep-set eyes radiating an agitation, his dry, crusted, quivering lips, and the extreme upset in his words: the underling was scared out of his wits.

'Whoa! Whoa! OK! One more step and you're out the door! Stop right there, old man, stop, STOP!'

'B-B-Buddy! Brother! Just hear me out...' Mohandas said, a little on the loud side, trying to calm things down a little. But there was too much desperation and not enough supplication in his voice, and things got worse. The man straightened his back and screamed, 'Get out! Stop right where you are or I'll rip you a new hole, old man! One more step and out on your arse!'

Hearing the shouting and screaming, four or five guys emerged from the office. They were dressed like higher-ups, and gave Mohandas the hard once-over.

'Who is this? How'd he get in here?'

'Where's security officer Pandey? He chews tobacco and sleeps on the job!'

'Who's on guard today at the main gate? Show me the log!'

'Get him out of here!'

'Isn't this peachy? Any old fart could sneak in, take out a gun and start shooting – *bang! bang!* – and then what? Set off a bomb maybe!'

'Hand 'em over to the police! Sharmaji, call the police, dial 1-0-0 on your mobile!'

Nobody was listening to Mohandas; he was just being pushed around in a shower of slaps, fists, and elbows raining on his head, back, shoulders, and face. Mohandas covered his head with his hands to protect his eyes, 'Please! Just hear me out, hey, stop hitting me, hey!'

Meanwhile, a small group of guards had come running. One was carrying a twelve gauge double-barrelled shotgun, the kind bank guards carry. The rest had batons. Shivers went up Mohandas's spine; stars from the new moon night on the banks of the Kathina flashed before his eyes, the celestial bodies screaming and groaning, then falling like shooting stars, breaking into pieces. A hard blow struck him unannounced and he let out a scream that sounded like a bound pig getting its throat slit. The sound reached the coal miners, who came out and gathered to watch the show.

(Pay attention, this story takes place at the same time as when that all-seeing Hindi guru was doing you-know-what to a woman in his ascetic quarters, and, thousands of miles and a few oceans away, the US president was sitting in a chair in the White House doing the same thing. When latter-day sea pirates dragged a descendant of Gilgamesh out from a hole near the Tigris and Euphrates where he'd hidden for his life, shining a flashlight in his mouth, counting his teeth, looking for a cyanide pill.

It was the time when the amount of power someone had was, by the law of a kind of backward ratio, equalled by the same degree to which that person had become out of control, violent, barbarous, hellishly immoral. And the same force applied to states, political organisations, castes, religious organisations, and individuals.)

Mohandas stood outside the main gate of the Oriental Coal Mines in the middle of the road. He'd simply stopped thinking. A frightful near-silence buzzed all around. He didn't realise he was standing in the middle of the street with trucks, Tempos, and cars honking their horns and whizzing by. He still had that thirty-rupee wallet in his pocket that he'd bought when he thought the job was his. In it was one hundred and seventy rupees, all from his labour and toil – this is what he had left, minus the sixty-five for his bus fare. Finding his wallet still there when he reached into his pocket, his mind eased a bit. He suddenly felt the sun's heat and moved quickly to the side of the road. He was hungry.

While eating at the Fatso's Vaishnava Pure Vegetarian Food Stall he found out that although there were two state transport buses only one private line had an evening service to the area near his village, Purbanra. He decided to take a look around Lenin Nagar, the coal miners' colony. He might see someone he knew, maybe someone he studied with at college, maybe someone else.

He lost his way in Lenin Nagar. It was afternoon, all of the apartment buildings looked alike, and everyone was at work in the mines. Only women and children were at home. A school bus was making stops and unloading schoolchildren who were walking on ahead. Lenin Nagar was an enormous residential colony. If I hadn't had the wool pulled over my eyes and been played for a fool, Mohandas thought, I would have been living in one of these flats with my family, bringing home a pay cheque; Devdas and Sharda would have been going to school wearing little uniforms and shoes and socks and getting off the school bus. We'd have a fan or cooler to help us sleep at night. But how totally ludicrous that in order to find out where Bisnath's flat was, he'd have to ask for his own name.

'Hi there friend, can you tell me where Mohandas lives?'

'Who? You mean supervisor sahib?'

'That's the one!'

'Go straight ahead, make a left at the fourth bylane, it's the third house, A/11, next to Dr Janardan Singh's flat.'

The door to the apartment was closed. The brass plate affixed to the wall outside read, 'Mohandas Viswakarma, Deputy Depot Supervisor, Oriental Coal Mines.'

He stood reading that for a little while before ringing the doorbell below the brass plate. The sound gave him a start since the hard ring was identical to the clerk's desk buzzer, the one that caused calamity.

A fourteen- or fifteen-year-old boy answered the door.

'Sahib's not at home, he just left for the market to go drink a lassi,' the boy said in one breath.

'Could I have a glass of water?'

Mohandas was very thirsty, the hot sun had been beating down on him, and the wind blew like a furnace. He was wilting. He'd been nicked and bruised on his face, arm, and back during his beating and subsequent ejection from the office compound, and the dried sweat was coagulating the blood in the cuts.

The boy looked him over head to toe.

'Wait here, I'll be right back.' He went inside.

Mohandas gulped down three glasses; the boy'd brought a cold bottle of water from the fridge. The water rejuvenated his body, brought the light back to his eyes, and calmed him. He noticed the boy's sympathetic look as he took the glass back.

'Who else is at home?' Mohandas asked.

'Nobody. Just Kasturi madamji. But she's sleeping. Come back after five.' When the boy started back in with the empty bottle, Mohandas said, 'When sahib comes back tell him that

Mohandas from Purbanra village stopped by. I'll come back this evening.'

The boy stopped. He looked quizzically at Mohandas. 'Who? Who should I say stopped by?'

'Mohandas!' Mohandas said a little louder, before slowly returning to the May inferno and the nearly melting pavement.

There wasn't much to Lenin Nagar market, though it ached for a modern makeover. There were a handful of dry-goods stores, a few convenience shops with some groceries. A Kaveri Fast Food that served dosas-idlis-vadas. Two food shacks with the usual tandoori, dhal makhini, kadhai paneer, butter chicken, aloo paratha. A liquor shop with whisky and local toddy with a sign outside that read, 'Cold Beer Available.' Two cigarette and paan stalls, and two stores with proper glass window displays that carried all sorts of plastic stuff, small electric appliances and electronics. Then another cavernous apparel store with a show window featuring crude foam mannequins modeling lacy bras and underwear that showed off everything.

Mohandas saw a police Tata Sumo parked in front of Lakshmi Vaishnav Restaurant, and among the handful of police inside drinking lassis was Vijay Tiwari from Mohandas's village, son of Pandit Chatradhari Tiwari, who'd been fixed up with a police inspector position by his in-laws.

Bisnath, too, was there.

Bisnath was having a good laugh at something as he finished his lassi; walking back toward the Sumo, Mohandas caught his eye. Bisnath did a double take, and for a moment the colour drained from his face. The laugh evaporated. Vijay Tiwari saw the panic on Bisnath's face and turned around to look; he was sitting in the driver's seat in full uniform.

Mohandas stood about fifteen yards away, beneath the lamppost, dressed in rags, scorched by the scalding wind.

A tense silence settled over the hot, sunny afternoon.

Bisnath climbed into the SUV. Vijay Tiwari started the engine and floored it, right at a terrified Mohandas, who stumbled to take cover behind a lamppost. Vijay Tiwari hit the brakes hard and the car ground to a halt right beside Mohandas; if it hadn't, the car would have smashed into Mohandas and the lamppost. He was in a daze.

'Get over here!' Vijay Tiwari called him over.

Not even eight years had passed since the very same Vijay Tiwari had studied with Mohandas at the M. G. Degree College. They had a class together and saw each other there every day. He'd been a bit slow in his studies. His father Pandit Chatradhari had held out Mohandas as a role model, since every year he was at the top of the class. Now the same Vijay Tiwari wore a police uniform, rode in a Tata Sumo fitted with cop sirens and a bullhorn, and put on a show: more than simply pretending he didn't know Mohandas, he put on a show of hostility and scorn. And why? Just because Mohandas was poor, low-caste? Or because he didn't have a job and was labouring quietly to support his family? Or maybe because these people had swindled him, walked all over what was rightfully his. But now, his presence threw a wrench into their freedom and carousing.

'You're lucky that lamppost was there otherwise you would've been dead meat!' Vijay Tiwari spat out.

'Eh, leave him be,' Bisnath said. 'It's not worth the mess just to swat a fly. And you, arsehole, had better not show your face around here again.'

Mohandas hadn't budged an inch from his spot.

Vijay Tiwari leant on the horn few times, and then flipped a switch to the bullhorn mounted on the roof of the SUV.

'Hey Bisnath!' the sound screamed from the loudspeaker. 'Have you lost your mind, Bisnath? Oh, Bisnath, what's the matter? Cat got your tongue? Gone deaf? BISNATH! Hey, Bisnath!'

They exploded into laughter inside the car.

'You didn't bring your wife with you, Bisnath? You came to die alone? Tsk, tsk.'

Bisnath climbed out of the car and went right up to Mohandas. He reached inside his pocket, took out a five hundred, and stuffed it into Mohandas's.

'From now on forget about your old name, and from now on don't even take a step toward Lenin Nagar. Today you got lucky. We were just drinking lassis. The lamppost saved your butt, otherwise you would've been a grease spot. If we ever see you around here again, it's into the coal furnace, and out as ash!' Then he turned towards Fatso's Vegetarian Restaurant and shouted, 'Nand Kishore! Hey! Can you bring a lassi to Bisnath over here? And make it cold, put some ice in it! It's Bisnath, from the next village over!' More laughter from inside the SUV.

Bisnath joined in, and while getting back into the car, whispered to Vijay Tiwari, 'Nand Kishore? Just a dhimar from Bhakhar who turned himself into a Brahmin after he came here and now runs a Vashniva vegetarian restaurant. Even married a brahmin girl from Sajanpur, the little weasel. Call him 'panditji' and he loves it, gets all swelled up with pride.'

'That's good! And so the brotherhood enlarges.' Vijay Tiwari chuckled at himself and turned to the food joint. 'Keep an eye on Bisnath, Panditji, and thanks for giving him a lassi to drink, and put it on my tab, and, oh, he's just a little off his rocker.'

'Don't worry yourself about it! Not one bit! All in a day's work! I'll put him back on his rocker!'

The Tata Sumo sped off, leaving Mohandas covered in a cloud of dust and exhaust.

He stood perfectly still, grabbing hold of the lamppost. Was this some movie where a scene had just wrapped up, and he was a character trapped inside? Or was it some twisted nightmare?

Fatty's Vaishnav Vegetarian Foodstop's light-skinned, beady eyed, middle-aged fat sweetmeat proprietor, Nand Kishore, held out a glass of lassi.

'Bisnath, oh Bisnath! Come and drink your lassi!'

Mohandas was leaving Lenin Nagar market and walking to the bus stand when he noticed a disturbed-looking man coming toward him. A little bag was slung over his shoulder, his pants were washed out, and coming apart at the seams. He came up to Mohandas and stopped.

'Do you know where Suryakant's flat is in Lenin Nagar, brother?'

Mohandas remembered seeing that name on a nameplate when he'd been looking for Bisnath's house. He tried to remember.

'Keep going straight ahead and you'll see Matiyani Chowk at the big intersection, and ask someone, it's not far from there.

The man started to leave and Mohandas asked him softly, 'Whose apartment are you looking for?'

'Suryakant's! From a village near Unnao.'

'What's the name of his village?'

'Gadhakola!'

'And what's your name'

The man hesitated. His lips trembled, his deep-set eyes began to well up, and in a thin, gravelly tone, a rough sound emerged.

'Suryakant! I'm Suryakant from Gakhakola!'

And with that he turned and shuffled toward Lenin Nagar.

(It's a story that takes place at the time when every government of every country on earth was promoting the same economic policies and playing the same political games, and when even the biggest billboard in the world can't cover up the massive chasm that has opened up between rich and poor.

It's the time when the revolutionary forces of the exploited and downtrodden from the early twentieth century were busy playing a game of chess to form coalition governments, lower the price of gas, and tighten their rule over the poor. And the time when a groundbreaking, historic consensus emerged among all parties in this twenty-first century postmodern democracy to cripple and crush all of the decent people of this country, the ones who get by with hard work and talent. Politics assumed the form of any means of power that's used to exercise control, perpetrate injustice, and oppress the citizenry.)

Mohandas returned home at eleven. Everyone had been eagerly awaiting his return. Kasturi had made rice, dhal, and an okra khuthima. She'd also stone-ground some green mango chutney.

Devdas and Sharda had already eaten and were asleep. Kaba was lying on the cot in the courtyard coughing away. 'Three times today he's spat up gobs of lung with the blood,' Kasturi informed him. Putlibai was sleeping next to him on the rug spread out on the floor beside the cot. Kasturi had waited to take her meal and still hadn't eaten; she ladled out his food and hers, then covered them with a lid.

Mohandas took off his clothes and wrapped himself in an angocha in order to wash up before eating; all the cuts and bruises were visible. The marks gave Kasturi a fright.

'What happened? Where did all those cuts come from?' she said, carefully examining his body with her hands. 'My god! These aren't just little scratches.' Mohandas quietly washed his hands and face, the cool water rinsing off the fatigue of the day, refreshing his whole body. Next to the washbasin was a good-sized jasmine plant in full flower; its scent filled the courtyard. He drew in a deep breath, filling his lungs with the sweet smell, closed his eyes for a moment, and incanted the name of his *satguru*, Kabir.

Kasturi removed the cover from the thali, releasing the smell of the rice into the courtyard. It was lohandi, an old stash Putlibai had put in the back of their rice bin and forgotten about, until today, when, remembering it, she groped around until she found the little bundle. Mohandas ate it with relish, and his fingers were covered in the mango chutney.

'The bisaindhi mango tree's bursting with fruit. We should get at least a couple of thousand for them, should I go pick and sell 'em tomorrow?' Mohandas said, before letting out a big burp to signal his satiety. 'You must do some kind of magic to make food taste as good as this! Mix together your mango chutney, rice and a good appetite, and that's what I call heaven!'

Kasturi's eyes welled up a little. She knew that another calamity had befallen Mohandas that day, one he'd keep hidden from her forever.

That night Kasturi instantly fell asleep after a long day and late night, but sleep didn't come to Mohandas for a while. He kept getting up, downing glass after glass of water. Some sort of storm was swirling around in his head, a terrible typhoon of disquiet.

Mohandas went to the Oriental Coal Mines once or twice more, but the trips turned out to be pointless since a rumour had been spread throughout Lenin Nagar that some loony popped up every couple of weeks claiming that he was the real depot supervisor, Mohandas, BA. Call him Bisnath and watch him go mad and say all sorts of crazy stuff.

He'd been defeated; Mohandas gave up on going to the coal mine. Day and night, he couldn't calm down. He stayed up all night by the sandy bank of the Kathina, quietly regarding the stars. In the village, Kabirpanthis were considered merely a low weaver or thatcher caste. Were they a scheduled caste or an adivasi or an aboriginal group? It was still unclear, according to the official government gazette. After the census ten years ago 'bamboo cutter' was tacked on to their caste description; on other papers 'Hindu' was indicated as their religion and 'Indian' for nationality. Their numbers were small, and none of them took any significant part in any of the political parties, never mind holding any government positions; so here too Mohandas became the butt of many jokes. The high-casters and rich folk asked him in passing, 'So, how's the job hunt going, Moh-hun-ah?'

'Take the job of looking after Vijay Tiwari's water buffalo,' someone advised him. 'At least you won't have to worry about putting a little bread on your plate. Make Kasturi happy, too. She wouldn't have to walk around barefoot.'

Others told him he should go visit Bisnath in Lenin Nagar, throw himself at his feet and offer to be his servant. Mohandas began to avoid the higher-ups of his village. He'd see them and get lost fast.

But it's not as if his fellow villagers didn't have any sympathy for him. Most of the people had genuine feeling for him, and wanted to help him out one way or another. But these were the same people who themselves were caught in some kind of fix. There wasn't one among them who had any real pull. They quietly did what they needed to do to get by with their own sweat and tears.

Ghanshyam was one of these. Though a Kurmi by caste, he wasn't poor. He had twenty acres of land, and had bought a tractor with a loan from the bank. He grew beans and vegetables and rented out his tractor. And yet it was still tough for him to meet his monthly bank payments of seven thousand. The market price for wheat and other crops about to be harvested was below cost in the market. A farmer named Bisesar from nearby Balbahra village had taken out a loan from the Grameen Bank in order to plant soya beans; a couple of months ago, in order to save his farm from auction, he climbed up a powerline, touched a live wire and died. Small farmers and farm workers were quitting village life and coming to the city in droves; this made Ghanshyam uneasy.

That day Mohandas had a slight fever. He'd been weaving baskets all day and all night, hauling water to the seedlings they'd planted, and was so tired that he'd fallen asleep without eating anything. When he woke up, he felt a little warm. He was still resting on the terrace when Ghanshyam came. He'd also brought Gopaldas, Kasturi's brother-in-law, along with him. The two of them told Mohandas that a friend of a friend of theirs knew the general manager of the Oriental Coal Mines, S. K. Singh. They told Mohandas to wash up and get dressed quickly and to catch the next bus to the mine. Ghanshyam and Gopaldas were nearly jumping out of their skins with excitement. They said that it was of the utmost importance that he go right away since the general manager was leaving to go on vacation the day after next. Gopaldas opened his bag and produced a pair of pants and shirt that he'd thought to bring with him. 'Put these on! You're not going to the manager looking like an old sack of bull's balls,' he said, and laughed along with Mohandas.

It proved not difficult at all to meet S. K. Singh, the general manager of the Oriental Coal Mines; the new shirt and pair of pants that Gopal had given Mohandas gave him a whole new level of confidence. He told S. K. Singh the whole story about how he'd come for the job interview on the eighteenth of August 1997, and had come in at the top of the list of candidates who were offered jobs; how on that day he deposited all his certificates and papers in the employment office, but never received the formal letter of offer; how Bisnath from Bichiya Tola had been working for five years having stolen Mohandas's name as depot supervisor, earning a monthly pay cheque of ten thousand. Ghanshyam had advised him not to mention when he'd gone to the mine to collect his papers and been beaten up at the behest of the clerks of the employment office, and was later threatened in Lenin Nagar by police inspector Vijay Tiwari.

S. K. Singh had an excellent reputation as a manager who

was on the level. If he did get mixed up in any funny business, it was merely due to his abiding fondness for a fine glass of whisky. Otherwise he was so on the level that he was capable of neither hurt nor help.

In any case, after listening to the story from beginning to end, the general manager summoned A. K. Srivastav, welfare manager of the Oriental Coal Mines, and instructed him to launch an enquiry, adding that he wanted a full report in a month's time when he returned from holiday. Mohandas was so moved by this development that he was on the verge of tears, silently incanting the names of Kabir and Malihamai.

The enquiry took place the following week. Welfare Officer A. N. Srivastav arrived at the apartment located at A/11, Lenin Nagar. Bisnath had got wind of the entire affair beforehand and there was nowhere he hadn't spun his web. He'd been living in Lenin Nagar under the name of Mohandas for five years, so everyone in the area knew him by this name. No matter who A. K. Srivastav asked what was the name of the person living in A/11, the answer was invariably 'Mohandas!' And the name of the man he himself had approved a loan from the welfare fund, and whom he'd himself known for over five years, was called 'Mohandas.' And the individual he saw in the office of the general manager, the man who called himself Mohandas – well, he had a hard time believing that someone who looked like that could be a college graduate. Srivastav had his doubts. Despite the clothing that Gopaldas had provided, years of hardship and penury and labour had imbued Mohandas with the look of a slightly demented illiterate. Enquiry officer Srivastav thought it over and concluded that it was possible that the depot supervisor was really someone else and had taken the name 'Mohandas,' but he couldn't believe that this person insisting he was the real Mohandas, could, in fact, be Mohandas.

Bisnath's preparations had been stunning. He rolled out the red carpet in welcome for Srivastavji. He instructed his wife Amita, who was wearing a low-cut top under her sari, to come into the living room with a tray of cool sherbet. Amita had gone to Lenin Nagar's newly-opened Shilpa Beauty Parlor for a full makeover. She commented while placing the tray on the table, 'You didn't bring sweet Sarita with you, sir?' He smiled, and the atmosphere instantly became intimate, homely, sensual. The enquiry officer's gaze was fixed on Amita's exposed midriff. Those days, fashion shows from Delhi and Mumbai were shown non-stop on the TV news. But this was a living model standing before him, not the TV news, but the real thing.

'Sir, this is my wife!' Bisnath announced holding out a plateful of munchies for Srivastav. 'Kasturi!'

'It sounds like a rather old-fashioned name, no?' the enquiry officer asked, picking up a cookie from a plate on the table rather than the munchies that'd been offered.

Amita, half laughing, gushed in, 'You see sir what happened was that the astrologer told father that a Pisces girl should have a name based in astrology even for her nickname. And then it was settled, that's why people also call me... oh, it's not important. They call me what they call me.'

'Oh! So Kasturi's your zodiac name?' he said, addressing Amita directly. 'Okay, so then what is the name people call you?' he asked, the grin growing wider, less formal.

Amita scrunched up her face in confusion, and didn't respond. Bisnath jumped right in.

'That's rich, Kasturi! Why be shy about giving your name?'

he asked with a chuckle. 'Fine, I'll tell him. Sir, I guess you could say her more common name, what we all call her at home, is Amita. Amita Bhardwaj.'

Enquiry officer Srivastav let out a grunt of laughter.

'You know, I'm always a little suspicious when ladies don't exhibit any modesty. Some femininity should be there, shouldn't it? I'll tell you what, Kasturiji. From now on I'll only refer to you as Amitaji! That is, if you don't object?'

'No sir, not in the least!' she warbled. 'But if you want to know the truth, whenever I hear someone calling me 'Amita' I think it's someone from my very own family.' She took a deep breath and let out a long sigh. 'The problem around here is that there's nobody like us. No one civilized, it's just these backward people, and for me it gets boring!'

'Naturally, it will take time to develop these people. There are plenty of projects here in progress for just that purpose. Two years ago what was there? Nothing.' Srivastav said matter-of-factly. 'So what do you do with yourself here in Lenin Nagar?'

'Not much, whatever I can, we ladies have our kitty parties, I'm on a couple of committees for helping out the poorest workers, I like working in social services.'

'And it's good that you do, very good. Sarita's got a deep interest in social services, too. You should come over to our place sometime, and see if you can bring Sarita on board.' By then Srivastav had completely forgotten what it was he'd come for.

Bisnath was smiling from ear to ear. Now was the moment. He said:

'It's like this, sir. Lenin Nagar's the kind of place where

91

everyone's suspicious and jealous of everyone else. There's no easy conversation or having a laugh with your neighbour. And now this much ado about nothing. Someone didn't get their way, so they found some perfect nobody, threw him a few peanuts, and next thing you know a complaint's been filed. I know who's been doing the meddling. There's a lot of caste business going on. Those people are breathing down our necks. I know exactly who's responsible for this funny stuff, but that doesn't matter. I'm not afraid of the truth. Please conduct your investigation without prejudice.'

'What is your father's name?'

'BABOOJI! O, babuji! Could you please come into the living room for a moment!' Bisnath said with a loud voice and a smile.

'It's just dumb luck that Amma-Babuji happened to come here yesterday. They'd made some pickle, and used that as an excuse to come by and see us! You should please ask my mother and father themselves their names.'

'Please excuse me,' Amita said, as her in-laws were about to enter. She then added in English, 'We're a traditional family.' She got up and left the living room.

Trailing behind Nagendranath as he entered the room was his wife, Renukadevi. Noticing the tilak piety marks affixed to their foreheads, Srivastav couldn't help but leaping from the couch and greeting them with a heartfelt *namaskar*. Then, words coated in honey, he asked, 'May I please know your full names? It's really just a bureaucratic formality, full names if you don't mind.'

Nagendranath didn't pause for a second: 'My name is Kabadas.' He reached inside his kurta and drew out a necklace. 'I took a vow and took this necklace and since then the verse of Tulsidas has been my guide and protection, and that's when I added 'das' to my name. And right here is my wife Putlidevi, Mohana's mother.' Renukadevi nodded her head in assent.

And thus, the enquiry was completed. Welfare Officer A. K. Srivastav's investigation concluded that all charges levelled against Mohandas, son of Kabadas, resident of Purbanra district Anuppur, Madhya Pradesh, were groundless. For clarification, he attached the certificates furnished by Purbanra chief Chatradhari Tiwari and the secretary of the municipality, Shyamala Prasad, to the report – certificates given to Srivastav by Bisnath himself.

At the behest of Bisnath and Amita – aka Mohandas and Kasturi – Srivastavji spent the rest of the afternoon relaxing with them at home, followed by an evening of first beer, then whisky, which was the run up to a scrumptious evening meal of desi chicken; and when, at eleven, it was time to get into his Maruti Zen and say goodbye, he continually asked Amita, whom he kept calling 'Kasturiji,' if she might, at his behest, come to their house and talk to his wife Sarita about getting more involved in social services.

But in spite of his being drunk, he kept his eyes fixed on Amita's midriff – in the dark of night, the flesh had grown magnificent and seeped deeply into his psyche.

(This occurred at the time when the director of the selection committee of the public service commission took millions in bribes and then installed thousands of his own government employees all over the state, and who went on the lam after a CBI raid; when suitcases full of banknotes arrived at the residences of top ministers under heavy security protection, while ordinary citizens were barred entry; when an inspector general in Haryana and a cabinet minister were arrested and charged with illegal activities with women, and murder; when the 'supercop' famous for killing underworld criminals in encounters turned out himself to be a hit man.

...at the time when, after making Hindi and Urdu the 'national languages' of the people of the subcontinent, individuals from powerful political organisations, claiming that they themselves were literary figures, formed committees for the establishment of anti-establishment Premchand, Neruda, Faiz, Nazrul-Nirala as the national writers of India.

...at the time when an ill, debt-ridden tailor, with no means left to support his family, poisoned his wife and two children to death, and was then caught trying to kill himself. He was imprisoned and charged under Indian Penal Code sections 302 and 309 for murder and attempted suicide.)

Mohandas had a breakdown after the report of the enquiry committee. Ghanshyam and Gopaldas met once more with the general manager A. K. Singh pleading with him for an additional enquiry, but he said that it's not how things worked to open a second enquiry. He said that the most capable and trustworthy officer had conducted the enquiry, and he didn't want to create any sense of doubt in him by ordering a repeat. Later it emerged that Bisnath and Amita had also begun to invite the general manager to their home to make sure he was well fed and had plenty to drink; his wife had also become active in 'social work' – and the kitty parties, where she would collect money for the next ladies' soirée, and keep a little for herself.

A rumour also spread in the coal mines that Amita had seduced A. K. Singh; his car was often spotted outside the gate of A/11 Lenin Nagar, home of coal mine supervisor Mohandas. People also began whispering that Bisnath, too, got involved; it seems that Singh sahib not only enjoyed partying, food, and drink, but men, too.

Mohandas had a breakdown, and smashed into smithereens. He couldn't eat or sleep, he worked absentmindedly. He was in a state of utter malaise, and all sorts of strange questions and doubts swirled through his mind. So, were all the people who had good jobs and held high positions and ran around in automobiles and caroused who they really claimed to be? The names people went by, was that who they really were? Or had they committed fraud and assumed the identity of others? Was anyone in Lenin Nagar authentic, with a real name, real father's name, place of birth? Or was everyone like Bisnath, chameleon-like, with many identities, counterfeit? Then Mohandas began to ask himself who, after all, he himself was? Mohandas or Bisnath? And the BA he earned from M. G. Degree College: had that been solely for Bisnath's benefit, too? Did it happen like this to everyone?

He looked high and low throughout the house for the old postcards sent to him from the government job office. He yelled and screamed at Kasturi when he couldn't find them. He did end up coming across a few postcards from a few years back with his name and his address. In town, people saw him and either didn't say anything, or told him he should approach some politician or high-ranking civil service officer about his case. But in his current state Mohandas was unable to do so. Even Pandit Chatradhari, head of Purbanra's village panchayat, had issued a written certificate declaring that Bisnath from Purbanra was Mohandas; his son, Vijay Tiwari, was in cahoots with Bisnath. He was always stealing glances at Kasturi and, like a hunter, he lay in wait for the day when a broken Mohandas would come fall at his feet and beg for the job at his buffalo dairy.

Mohandas kept noticing that whenever a public water pump was approved by the local panchayat it'd be installed right outside the home of one of the more important people in the village. When teachers were hired, or slots opened up for female teachers or rural health workers, or grants became available for building houses under the Indira Awas program, or funds were released by the Grameen Development Department for digging wells or tilling land, when the Nehru Employment Program had openings in its program for the educated unemployed, those same people would be the ones to divvy up the spoils. Sharda and Devdas reported that the same kind of discrimination happened during lunchtime at school when they ladled out the gruel.

That night for the first time in years Mohandas went over to his childhood mate Biran Baiga's house; they got some stiff mahua brew and made a pork curry. Gopaldas also came. The group of four or five began drinking at seven. They'd also got hold of a dholak and a pair of manjira. That day Mohandas had got paid by the Seth from Vindhyachal Handicrafts for the bamboo ware he'd made: twelve hundred rupees. Gopaldas also had a bulging wallet. Biran Baiga was hosting, but the money for the liquor and meat had come from Mohandas. The stuff that Biran's wife and sister brewed was so strong, it'd burst into flames if you rubbed it against the wall.

In the soulful music, Mohandas and his friends forgot

about their sorrows for a little while. Bihari played the dholak, Parmode the manjira. Mohandas, buzzed and feeling good, sang:

Hello mister train man where are you driving your train?
Tell me where you drive your train
And I'll tell you where you can find me and mine
Tell me your name, your village, where I can find you
Love pushes love along the tracks
Only news about love reaches us way out here
Love makes us dance, our bodies spin, whirl
in this town that's as conjured up as love, the mirage
Here's my address, what's yours?
How can I reach you, mister train driver?

It was two in the morning by the time the women served dinner. Everyone was ravenous. Biran's sister had used mustard oil to prepare the pork with spices, garlic, onions; the smell filled the entire courtyard. Everyone helped themselves to a roti and dug in. There was also a big pot of rice. Mohandas, however, was silent. It was as if the singing had stuck a little needle in him; he felt a stitch in his chest that he tried to suppress and forget about by drinking more than the rest.

With a handful of food he was about to scoop into his mouth, Mohandas stopped, looked over everyone, and then looked at them once more; a sob then emerged, followed by uncontrollable weeping. Gopaldas, Biran, Bihari and Paramodi were so hungry and it'd been so long since they'd had such a good meal that they were a little bit offended at Mohandas's outburst. Taking bite after bite of food, they asked while chewing, *What's the matter? Why don't you eat first?*

Mohandas wiped away his tears and asked Biran Baiga, 'Who are you? What's your name?'

'Biran. Biran Baiga,' Biran said with a laugh.

'And your father? What's his name?' Mohandas continued.

'My father's name is Dind-wa Baiga,' he responded, still laughing. 'And you're drunk on the ma-hoo-wa.'

Everyone thought that was funny. Mohandas's eyes were bloodshot. He plonked his fingerful of food down on the tin thali and raised his voice:

'Biran, Parmodi – tell me if you can, who am I? And don't just feed me lines or treat me like an idiot. I want all of you to swear on Malihamai!'

'You are Mohandas, your father is Kaba, and your mother is Putli,' Biran said firmly, poking Mohandas in the chest with the finger he'd been eating with. The group began laughing. Mohandas didn't respond but regarded Biran for a moment before staring down the rest of the group. He wanted to put a stop to his fears about whether these people were who they said they were, or some other people. Then the feeling crept in that they were to a man quite real people who'd been, like him, cheated out of something and, they too, had had the rug pulled out from under them. The only difference was that he'd found out the secret, whereas the rest of them were still in the dark.

Mohandas wanted to instruct his childhood friends to go to government offices, go to skyscrapers and mansions and coal mines and factories in the cities, and to Lenin Nagar, Gandhi Nagar, Ambedkar Nagar, Shastri Nagar, and other residential colonies like them and ask around to see if some imposter has deprived them of their rights and is living there saying that they are them, their father is his father, and they're from where he is from. But even though he was buzzed he felt that if he told them this they'd just say he was drunk.

His four friends were busy eating. Biran's wife Sitiya and his sister Ramoli joined them. The two had also been drinking the mahua, and it was all frolic and fun with them, laughing and joking and eating. Mohandas, however, had by then separated from the group, and sat in the corner alone where he'd taken the bottle with him, letting out little sobs between singing verses of Kabir and taking swigs from the bottle.

It was four in the morning when his mates slung Mohandas over their shoulders and took him home. It was the first time Kasturi had seen her husband in this kind of shape. She began castigating Gopaldas and Biran until Gopaldas handed her a thousand rupees and said sorrowfully, 'I kept saying you've had enough, you've had enough, but he wouldn't listen. Take this, it's the money that fell out of his pocket.' That quieted her.

It was seven in the morning when Kabadas started with a fierce coughing fit, as if a tornado were stuck in his throat. It showed no sign of abating. Blind Putlibai ran around crazed, like a cow broken loose from its tether. Her cries echoed through the neighbourhood; Kasturi awoke, and tried to shake Mohandas awake. But he was still drunk with mahua and showed no signs of consciousness. She poured a bucket of water over him, causing him to open his eyes. They were as red as if soaked in blood. He was still intoxicated. She screamed, 'Get up! Go run get a doctor! His cough is deathly!'

Men, women, and children from the village began coming over. Devdas and Sharda stood panicked beside their grandfather's bed. It was as if his insides had exploded; each cough

99

came with spit full of blood and flesh. Lines of ants began forming on the ground; horseflies began swarming.

Everyone tried to shake the drunken sleep out of Mohandas. It was no easy task, but he finally began steadying himself with his hands and lifting himself up; everything looked terrifying through those bloodshot eyes. He didn't recognise a soul, and he couldn't focus. Then suddenly a big grin came over his face. He struggled with all his might to look directly at the man he recognised, Ramai Kaku. Mohandas's voice came out like gravel: 'Kaku, who am I, what's my name, Kaku, tell me, tell me!' Mohandas then collapsed on the spot into a lifeless heap.

The wails and cries of the village women rose, and Putlibai's were the loudest. Soon it was a kind of harmony of women's lament.

Kabadas died. The flies covered the bamboo and cutter under his cot. He'd been up half the night shucking bamboo and it was only yesterday they'd received an order from Vindhyachal Handicrafts to make thirty baskets and fifty winnows.

That morning around seven thirty the cat had pounced on and gobbled up the pair of myna birds out in the open of Kasturi's room. Mama myna was carrying two eggs in her belly; crushed feathers and drops of blood still littered the earthen floor of the room; the day before Kasturi had covered it with cow dung.

Mohandas, who had been left passed out in the courtyard, wasn't conscious enough to be aware of how his father's funeral rites were conducted; he wasn't there to witness how village and caste elders took Kaba's body to the cremation ground, how Mohandas's mother Putlibai kept rapping her forehead on his cot and how she cried while she cleaned his blood and spit from the mattress, basket, and water jug; how little Devdas took the place of his father and lit his grandfather's cremation pyre, and how his childhood friend Biran Baiga performed the kapal-kriya, the ceremonial breaking of the skull. Mohandas knew nothing of this. The low-caste gosain priest shook Kasturi down for five hundred rupees, and the forest guard took another five hundred for himself; the wood he used from Patera for Kaba's pyre wasn't even dry. All the money Gopaldas had given Kasturi was gone.

Mohandas snored with vigour. He opened his eyes a couple of times, looked around as if he had been brought someplace he didn't recognise, then went back to sleep. Maybe it was the deep sleep, or maybe the mahua had been adulterated with lentina or besharm leaves, or maybe it was the pork curry that'd been bad. But if any of these had been the case, Biran, Parmodi, Bihari, Kitiya, and Ramoli would've have come down with something. But they'd all been fine, and what was more, as soon as Kaba died, they all busied themselves arranging for wood, going to Khanda village to tell the gosain what had happened, and making sure all the funerary arrangements were made properly. Mohandas's drunkedness wasn't an ordinary one.

'The mahua's flooded his brain. Mix jeera and ajwain with yogurt and spoon it in his mouth!' Biran Baiga advised.

Kasturi mixed the jeera and ajwain in a little cup and brought it over to Mohandas; Gopaldas took Mohandas's head in his lap. Mohandas's eyes and mouth opened, and he regarded the two as if he had no idea who they were. In a weak and barely audible voice he asked Kasturi, 'Who are you, sister? And who am I, tell me!' He then smiled at Kasturi and began humming:

101

Hey Bilaspur lovely
I'm a Raigarh lad
Don't you think we're made for each other?

This was too much for Kasturi, and she began to break down. Sharda also began to cry at her father's condition. Gopaldas patted Kasturi on the shoulder, took the little cup from her hand and told Mohandas, 'Here, take your medicine.'

Mohandas looked at him sheepishly, as if he himself were a little child, drew the cup to his mouth, and drank it in one gulp. Maybe somewhere in his mind stirred the wish to get better. Kasturi and Gopaldas were relieved; maybe it would make a difference – otherwise, they'd have to call the doctor.

Mohandas fell back asleep.

Mohandas slept in the same spot in the same corner of his house for five days and four nights nonstop. The word had spread in the village that he'd completely lost his mind and he didn't recognise a soul anymore, not even his wife and kids. Some had it that the mahua he'd drunk had been diluted with urea, while others insisted that his summer-heat-induced faint at the Oriental Coal Mines that day had erased his memory. Vijay Tiwari spread a rumour that his spotted dog had bitten Mohandas by accident, *and now you'll see, as sure as the sun will shine, Mohandas will start barking like a doggie.* Everyone had his own rumour. It was tough for Devdas and Sharda; they went to school and were asked by the teacher and kids, *Is your papa a loony toon? Does he even know who you are anymore? Is it true he only sleeps and sleeps – and if so, how does he bathe and pee and poo?*

A rumour even spread that one night Mohandas got up in the middle of the night, grabbed his father's machete, and ran around trying to slash and kill everyone in the house. Kasturi tackled him and blind old Putlibai tied him up with a rope, otherwise god knows what might have happened!

(All of this was happening at exactly the same time as when the 'India Shines' campaign was in full force, and the finance minister and World Bank promised that as long as the five point eight per cent rate of economic growth that started in 1990 continued for the same number of years, India would become the United States, given the fact that the US became the US in fifty years with half that rate of growth.

... it was the time when I was diagnosed with bone tuberculosis, two of my lumbar discs in a state of advanced degeneration. I was confined to bed for nine months and the smiling heads of the Buddhas carved from the Bamiyan mountains in Kandahar were being destroyed by rocket fired missiles...

... it was the time when four years' worth of the sweat of destitute workers, nineteen thousand tons of steel, and four hundred and fifty seven thousand cubic metres of earth were moved during the construction of Asia's biggest, and the world's most expensive and modern, metro rail system... At the time when the houses and homes and fields and yards of more than fifty million adivasis and dalits and aboriginals were submerged under water for the construction of thirty five hundred dams... At the time when twenty million people living in India didn't have drinking water... and seven hundred million didn't have a place to wash, bathe, piss, or shit.

... it was the time when the parties in the Left coalition raised hell in the streets of Delhi to protest against a rise in gas prices, when some ninety percent − nine hundred and twenty million Indians − never bought a drop of gas in their lives...

… it was the time when the police fired on and killed a dozen starving farmers in Ganganagar and Tonk in Rajasthan because they'd thrown rocks demanding water to irrigate their withering crops…

… it was the time when Abdul Karim Telgi ran a counterfeit postage stamp operation worth billions of rupees, with several high-ranking politicians and officials working in cahoots. It was the time when an elderly critic of Hindi letters proclaimed that a bureaucrat-turned-writer was the new Muktibodh, and a second old corrupt critic insisted that some paper pusher was Premchand and Phanishvarnath Renu reincarnate and rolled into one. It was the time when the atom bomb blew up at Pokhran and the Goodwill Bus was running between India and Pakistan after the Kargil war.

And it was the time when the waters of the Kathina river were exacting revenge in Purbanra for the paper mill and the rotting wood at the dam by inundating the land where Mohandas had planted his cucumbers and watermelon and honeydew…

The land where Mohandas, crying 'hu tu tu!' had played with Kasturi in the strong current of the Kathina, the memory of their hot passion under the glow of the starry night was the birth, nine months later, of Sharda…)

The truth was that Mohandas wasn't crazy, and nothing was wrong with his memory. The blow to his psyche had silently festered during the week of unbroken sleep, stupor, and drunkenness. When he awoke, he was again the same Mohandas: a person who knew full well that he and only he was the real Mohandas, son of Kaba, resident of Purbanra, district Anuppur, Madhya Pradesh, who had, some ten years ago, earned a BA from

M. G. Degree College, and was second in his class. He was the Mohandas who'd been denied a job because he had no connections, no pull, and no money to use for bribes. He wasn't a member of any gang or group or mafia because he didn't belong to a caste that had any power. He knew full well that he and countless others like him had been cheated and lied to and tricked for many, many years, but he had no means to do anything about it.

And one other thing that he knew full well was that Bisnath from Bichiya Tola, son of Nagendranath, who'd assumed the guise of Mohandas Vishwakarma, son of Kabadas, and who was pulling in ten thousand a month as a depot supervisor at the Oriental Coal Mines, was in no way, shape, or form Mohandas. No, he was a soulless bastard, a dyed-in-the-wool caste fascist, and a fraud who wielded so much power that Mohandas, compared to him, was nothing more than a sick, whimpering little mouse.

Mohandas knew that his father – the real Kabadas – had died of TB, after coughing up bloody phlegm while making bamboo baskets, mats, and winnows; but he didn't have the capability to prove this, since Bisnath's father Nagendranath was still living as Kabadas in Lenin Nagar and Bichiya Tola – and he was the one who had the papers to prove it.

Mohandas's silence grew every day. The dam on the Kathina had taken away one of his livelihoods, so he began working at Imran's Star Computer Centre as a typist, and making printouts and copies. His son Devdas began working at the roadside Durga Auto Repairing Works, helping repair flat tires and fix whatever car problems he could with a screwdriver and wrench. He made one or two hundred rupees a month, enough to cover his school costs. It'd been two years since Sharda had quit working as a nanny for Bisnath's kids and doing their household chores; Renukadevi had gone to Lenin Nagar to live with her husband. A year ago, Sharda got work in town at the Aishwarya Beauty Parlor. Shikha Madam was crazy about Sharda and helped her out with school. She said, 'Sharda, one day you'll become a model and then Miss World and you'll be on TV!' Sharda, who was eight, dreamed every night that this would come true.

Kasturi kept an eye on people's crops in addition to working in the fields of neighbours and villagers. Putlibai's knees had turned to stone after Kabadas's death, and she could no longer walk. In order to relieve herself, she had to crawl on all fours out back, and then come back to her corner where she sat on her burlap-like mat. Her blindness had grown even more severe.

It was in the Star Computer Centre that Mohandas met Harshvarddhan Soni. He'd come there to have some photo-copies made for his legal practice, and to have some letters typed. By then, Mohandas was a fast typist and made few mistakes. He told his whole story to Harshvarddhan right then and there.

Toward the latter part of the twentieth century, I'd spent a couple of decades as an active member of a particular ideological political party; Harshvarddhan Soni had been in the same party. His life had also been full of the same struggles and sorrows, vic-tories and defeats. The son of a woman who was a middle school teacher, Harshvarddhan was, from the beginning, independent-minded and quite perceptive. His older brother, Srivarddhan Soni, had come in first in his BA class for engineering; despite the degree, however and after the joblessness got worse and worse, one night, five years ago, he'd tied a rope to the ceiling fan and hanged himself. The tragedy of his brother's suicide made such a deep impact on Harshvarddhan, son of a shopkeeper and middle school teacher, that even during his studies he began participating in the student wings of political organisations. He married outside of his caste, and was punished for doing so by being expelled from it.

Harshvarddhan Soni then earned an LLB and made his living working alongside his party in the local court on legal matters. When Mohandas told him the story that day at the Star Computer Centre – it wasn't really a story, but a real account of a living life – he decided to take his case and seek redress in court.

'How much money do you have at the moment?' Harshvarddhan asked, looking at Mohandas's patched-up shirt and washed out jeans. 'I'll take your case, and you will receive justice.'

Mohandas's eyes lit up, and his frail body began trembling. For an instant he didn't believe that it was possible someone would aid him like this.

'Right now I have eighty rupees,' he answered. 'In a few days I'm supposed to get forty more. And Imran pays me a couple of hundred in wages.'

Harshvarddhan calculated that Mohandas at most could be counted on for five hundred a month, while it took in the vicinity of five thousand in court fees just to have the case heard. The economic policies of one government after the next transformed India's big cities into little Americas, while putting people who lived in the same country into the poorhouse, but in tiny villages and undeveloped places, and creating countless Ethiopias, Ghanas, and Rwandas. A professor who toed the ideological line of a connected political party made around fifty thousand a month in Delhi-Lucknow, Mumbai-Bhopal, Kolkata-Patna, and a no-name freelancer could expect five hundred to a thousand rupees for a two page piece; but the hardworking, industrious Mohandas, from the wrong side of the tracks from a forgotten village, and those like him, took a whole month to scrape together four hundred.

Harshvarddhan realised that he himself would have to find the funds if Mohandas were to have his day in court. He put in a thousand of his own money, asked friends for another two thousand, and got the rest from the charity fund of the Lions Club – in other words, he was able to get the cash.

Slowly but surely, one way or another, judge (first class) Gajanan Madhav Muktibodh, who preferred his bidis to smoking cigarettes, who was thin as a stick, whose bony cheeks jutted out, whose brow was scored with countless wrinkles, agreed to hear the case of Mohandas in his court of law.

Mohandas, s/o Kabadas, caste Vishwakarma, r/o Purbanra, district Anuppur, M. P. versus Vishwanath, s/o Nagendranath, caste Brahmin, r/o Bichiya Tola, currently r/o A/11 Lenin Nagar, Oriental Coal Mines, district Durg, Chhattisgarh.

The moment the court went into session, S. K. Singh, the chief executive of the Oriental Coal Mines, along with welfare officer A. K. Srivastav, along with other senior execu-tives, were summoned before the court to testify and explain how and why it was that the man who had been working for five years as deputy depot supervisor known as Mohandas Vishwkarma was, in fact, Vishwanath (s/o Nagendranath, r/o Bichiya Tola).

Judge Gajanan Madhav Muktibodh ordered the district magistrates of Anuppur and Durg to launch an official enquiry into the matter and instructed them to report their findings to the court within two weeks' time.

The court order and summons by bidi-smoking judge G. M. Muktibodh created chaos in the Oriental Coal Mines. The local newspapers ran the headline:

WHO IS THE REAL 'MOHANDAS'?

Anil Yadav and Khalid Rashid – local reporters for NDTV and Aajtak national news channels – sent clips of the story to Delhi and Bhopal, but it didn't fit into the 'National Scene' or 'Indian Panorama' segments, and didn't even made the 'Regional News' because the story didn't include any big politicians or bigwigs from the big cities of Delhi-Bhopal-Lucknow.

(This is a story from the time when Vidhu Vinod Chopra's 'Munna Bhai MBBS' was making a killing at the box office. George Bush and Tony Blair had both been re-elected and were returned to power, and Saddam Hussein, his beard giving him the look of a crazed fakir, face covered with wrinkles, was writing poetry in an American prison, and former Indian Prime Minister V. P. Singh, who instituted the recommendations of the controversial Mandal Commission that set aside job and school slots for the lower-castes, was diagnosed with cancer, his kidneys were failing, he was on dialysis – just like J. P. had been – and was quietly painting oil canvases in a corner of Delhi.

It was the time when the district collector from Patna, Bihar – Gautam Goswami – whose photo was on the cover of *Time* as a hero when the big floods hit that year, later made off with tens of millions of rupees from the flood fund; and it was the time when the new government constituted a new film censor board, and placed at its helm a nawab from a royal family, former captain of the Indian cricket team, but who was unable to delete a scene in a film where he was caught red-handed hunting the endangered black buck and other animals...

It was the time when for fifteen years running each and every vacant position connected with a Hindi language post was filled with a son, a son-in-law, a daughter, a father-in-law, an arse kisser, or a right-hand man of a search committee member, right out in the open, without shame, without any CBI inquiry or any questions asked in the Rajya Sabha or Lok Sabha.

It was a time when the Human Resources Minister had transformed the public sector into a machine for corruption that churned out thinkers, pedagogues, sociologists, novelists, historians, intellectuals, artists, teachers... and the political battle to capture the minds and hearts of the youngsters was on, by endlessly re-writing and re-re-writing history texts and schoolbooks.

It was the time when India ranked seventh among the world's most corrupt countries, sixth among nuclear-armed nations, second in population, while in poverty Bangladesh was at the top.)

Both Harshvarddhan Soni and Mohandas were confident that the court of the judge G. M. Muktibodh would separate milk from water and sort out right from wrong. They were confident for two reasons. The first was based on the fact that the magistrate smoked bidis and drank strong chai from the streets, and there was no sign at all he was looking to have his palms greased. The man was not corrupt.

The second reason was that truth was in Mohandas's corner: he was the real Mohandas, BA.

'These lies will come crashing down like a house of cards! Like the light of dawn, all will be revealed! Victory to Malihamai! Please let it be so, Kabirguru!' Kasturi's gloomy life was once again sprouting shoots of hope. Though Putlibai's blindness had grown even more severe since Kabadas's death, she still sat on an old mat in the corner, like an ancient hawk with clipped wings, her ear forever trained toward the inner rooms of the house.

And so one morning at the crack of dawn, while Mohandas was eating his breakfast of leftover rice and potatoes and getting ready for his appearance in court, the rapturous voice of Putlibai suddenly echoed throughout the house. She chirped like a merry-making bird,

'Little one! Devdas! Come quick and take a peek in the living room! I think the myna bird's made herself a new nest, what do you think? Come quick!'

Mohandas was trying to finish his food as fast as he could so that he could get to court early; people had warned him that the judge who puffed mightily on his bidis was a stickler for starting on time. Five minutes late and he'd bump the case being heard to the following day and start straightaway on the next.

As he wolfed down his breakfast of stale rice and potatoes that'd have to last him the whole day, his blind old, bird-like mother sang out in a rapturous voice:

Sing the song of satguru
Sing the song of satguru
Sing the song of satguru and set your soul free

The chief executive of the Oriental Coal Mines, S. K. Singh, was not present in court. His lawyer was there to plead

111

on his behalf. The company welfare officer A. K. Srivastav had brought his complete enquiry file with him, and gave it to the judge for his perusal, along with all supporting documents. Harshvarddhan Soni was deflated: of the three witnesses from Bichiya Tola he'd called to testify that the man who had been working at the Oriental Coal Mines for several years as a junior depot manager was their childhood friend Vishwanath, not Mohandas, two of them didn't show up, and the third, Dinesh Kumar Sahu turned into a hostile witness and testified in front of the packed courtroom that Vishwanath was the real Mohandas. Then he pointed his finger at Harshvarddhan Soni and Mohandas and claimed that the two of them had one month ago come to his house and told him that they'd give him five thousand rupees for telling the court what they told him to say.

Judge Gajanan Madhav Muktibodh set the next hearing for one month's time; Harshvarddhan and Mohandas were stunned.

They now pinned all their hopes on the report of the district magistrates. If Mohandas was going to get justice, it could only be when the truth came forward.

Harshvarddhan and Mohandas were speechless when, during the following court session, the reports of the district magistrates of Durg and Anuppur were presented. The investigations found that charges regarding the name and identity of Mohandas s/o Kabadas, deputy depot collector at the Oriental Coal Mines, were baseless. According to reliable testimony, circumstantial evidence, and after questioning several members of the grameen and panchayats, it was indisputably proven that Mohandas was Mohandas, and not Vishwanath.

Later they found out that Vishwanath had dropped ten thousand on the patwaris of the two districts, Durg and Anuppur, plus some hard liquor and spicy chicken. None other than Vijay Tiwari had picked up Bisnath in his police vehicle and helped him deliver the bribes to the patwaris. In any case, that was the real meaning of an inquiry headed by the collector, aka district magistrate, aka zilla adhikari: in the fine tradition of the administrative services, the inquiry was pawned off onto the lowly patwari. Whenever a court ordered a collector to make an inquiry, the collector would take note of the order, then send it to his subordinate, the SDM. The SDM would entrust the task to the tehsildar, who would order the sub-tehsildar to take care of it. That's how it went, from the revenue inspector, aka IR, aka qanungo, until it finally landed in the lap of the patwari, who, finally, was the collector's eyes and ears.

Bisnath and Vijay Tiwari handed over the stack of hundreds to Kamal Kishore, patwari of Bichiya Tola and Purbanra, plus a bottle of Macdowell's No. 1 whisky, and butter chicken, and mutton seekh kabab – Kamal Kishore fell at the men's feet in gratitude.

'Have I ever let you down before? All this cash – Jesus and Krishna! With all this money I'll turn a mouse into a moose, a club into a spade, a farm into a freeway!' the patwari said all dreamy, jumping for joy while stuffing the money into his bag. He downed a triple of the Macdowell's No. 1 in one shot, and just like that, right then and there, without moving an inch, the problem had been thoroughly investigated; the one-page white paper – a most official report – was readied, and the inquiry conducted by the district collector into the matter of Mohandas versus Vishwanath was completed in under fifteen minutes.

To put it another way, this rust-eaten steel frame of bureau-cracy that had been readied for power by the English over subservient India had just transformed Bisnath, s/o Nagendranath, into Mohandas, s/o Kabadas.

Mohandas again broke down. He incanted the name of Kabir non-stop. He sat for hours in front of the little shrine to Malihamai. She only took the thickest, sweetest cream as an offering. And only from goat's milk at that. High casters didn't frequent her shrine. The thakurs, baniyas, babhnan, and lalas had their own gods and goddesses. Gosains, rather than brahmins, conducted her puja. It was said that brahmins who had shared food with dalits or adivasis, or who married them were called gosains in their own caste community.

Mohandas went to Khanra village and found Siu Narayan Gosain, and gave him twenty rupees and an uncooked mixture of dhal, rice, turmeric, and gur, with which he performed a puja to Malihamai; he also made an offering of a full half pound of fresh goat's milk cream to the goddess.

Something else happened in the meantime. One morning at dawn, Kasturi was out in the fields doing her morning toilet with a couple of other women from the village. There was some commotion behind the bushes, as if someone was hiding.

For her own safety, Kasturi had taken to tucking a little scythe into her the waist of her trousers; she knew all too well that even after giving birth to two kids she was still the loveliest woman of the village. As long as she could remember she'd been subjected to the vulture-like stares of the local Brahmin slimeballs.

Kasturi stood up from her squat and removed the scythe from the cloth at her midriff. Holding it in her hand she approached the bush carefully; Ramoli, Sitiya, Chandna and Savitri followed.

'Hey, now's who's that hiding behind the bush? Come on out, I'll cool you down, you cunt wipe! What are you scared of, arse breath!' screamed Kasturi. The rest of the women surrounded the bush, each with a lota in hand for washing their potties.

Chatradhari's son Vijay Tiwari dashed out from behind the bush and ran off. His flabby body looked like a chubby watermelon as he scampered away in his boxers and undershirt.

Kasturi chased him for a bit, knife in hand. Ramoli, Sitiya and Savitri hurled their potty lotas after him. Inspector Vijay Tiwari ran as fast as he could, stumbling and tripping. The women screamed after him:

'Call the TV station! They'll get some great clips!'

'Run away, run away! Big boy inspector is making fudge in his pants!'

Vijay Tiwari was now scared through and through. Who knows what kind of nonsense Mohandas and his lawyer Harshvarddhan Soni might cook up and publish in the papers or get shown on TV?

(All of this was happening at the time when, for the first time in Asian political history, an Indian woman was made member of the communist party politburo, while another woman kicked away the chair of the prime minster's post.

It was the time when three non-stop giggling women were appointed members of the jury of the most important film festival where Ritwik Ghatak's *Subarnarekha* or *Kamol Gandhar* or Shailandra's *Teesri Kasam* were never even shown.

It was the time when a female US soldier working at Abu Ghraib prison stripped Iraqi prisoners naked and made them climb on top of one another to form some kind of pyramid, and then draped them with the American flag.

115

It was the time when power was defining gender.

It was the time when a girl from the north-east of India was kidnapped into a car near Dhaula Kuan in Delhi and raped for two-and-a-half hours nonstop by five men while travelling on every VIP road in Delhi. And it was when in Imphal, after the rape and murder of Manorama, hundreds of Krishna-devotee women stripped naked in front of the army headquarters to protest.

It was the time when two women failed in their struggle against the Sardar Sarovar dam, and so four thousand dalit and adivasi homes and fields and yards were submerged, and in the flood, forest animals and plants and trees and so much more was swept away.

The sad faces of those tired women were shown on TV, nonstop, in tears, defeated.

It was the time when I left Delhi and moved to Vaishali and from my rooftop could see that very same Jhandapur in Ghaziabad where exactly fifteen years earlier the revolutionary artist and performer named Safdar Hashmi was murdered.)

In the court of Gajanan Madhav Muktibodh, judge (first class), all the witnesses and evidence – and even the two investigative reports of the two district magistrates' inquiries – corroborated that Bisnath was indeed Mohandas. So, then: this pauper who's in a bad way and who swears and swears he's Mohandas – who is he? This court didn't have any direct judicial authority over this question. It possibly could be another case altogether, if some lawyer submitted a petition on behalf of the plaintiff.

Harshvarddhan Soni couldn't sleep for three days and three nights. He positively knew that Mohandas was Mohandas – but it wasn't just that this was difficult to prove, it was becoming impossible. He sent me an email:

'This is too much. I can't eat, I can't sleep. Neither can Mohandas. Everybody knows he's the real Mohandas, but it's impossible to prove. I'm at my wits' end. I don't know what to do. The two of us are receiving threats: *shut up or else.* In the meantime I found out that Bisnath has taken on Ras Bihari Rai as his attorney. You know him as well as I do – big shot in the ruling party. His wife's a member of the city council and is the head of a few government organisations and NGOs. There are half-a-dozen people ready to testify on behalf of Mohandas: Biran Baiga, Gopaldas, Biharidas, Ramoli, Sitiya… but their appearance will make it seem like they're witnesses we just bought off… each one of them looks like a homeless person.

'What I'm thinking is that I'll go straight to the judge and have a word with him. He smokes bidis and looks a little, well – off. His name is G. M. Muktibodh. He's Marathi, but he speaks Hindi like you wouldn't believe. After court lets out he sits outside drinking chai at Ramdeen's little tea shack on the side of the road.

'And I've noticed that in court when he looks at Mohandas, there's something in his eyes that stirs a little bit and makes him nervous. The veins on his forehead get bulgy and they look like they're going to pop out of his head. I'm actually a little scared that they might one day burst. There's something in his eyes that reminds me of a spy or secret agent who can very quietly see deeply into anyone's soul, like he can probe and pierce anything. The word is that his house is filled with books and he reads and reads every night until three in the morning.

'I've also heard something else that's a little disturbing, that even though G. N. Muktibodh is a judge of the first class, the government's got the CID watching his every move...'

With no other option he could think of, Harshvarddhan Soni took what amounted to a gamble. Any time a lawyer decided to meet a judge about an ongoing case, and on top of this with a judge with an air of mystery – it's a decision fraught with danger. If G. M. Muktibodh got angry, Harshvarddhan could jeopardise his entire career. His past had been full of every possible struggle, strain, and sorrow; the memory of the suicide of his despondent brother who couldn't find work never left his mind for a moment. 'The practice of law' was just a bunch of words. Most of the people who came to him didn't have enough money for a fancy lawyer. He wasn't going to see a cent from Mohandas's trial, and had even put in five thousand of his own money on the case. And yet – he decided to take the risk and go and meet the judge.

Harshvarddhan felt a little hopeful when he arrived at the door of Gajanan Madhav Muktibodh's flat and saw on his face an expression as if he'd already known he was coming, that he knew absolutely positively that Harshvarddhan was planning on paying him a visit. He pulled up a rickety old wooden stool and said, 'Have a seat! I'll go make some tea,' and disappeared into the kitchen.

Harshvarddhan glanced around the room. Everything was scattered everywhere. Piles of books lay all around, some of them kept open with pencils, cards, or leaves stuck in the spine. Maybe he was fond of those particular pages and had to read them over and over. The condition of the room suggested that he lived alone. Harshvarddhan had found out that the judge had been transferred frequently from one undeveloped area to another, ones with many adivasis, where cases like this were rare: cases where big shots or rich businessmen or people at that level might see any grief. Harshvarddhan saw portraits of Gandhi and Marx on the wall. A small Ganesh statue was kept in the corner. Bookshelves against the left wall were filled with law books that looked as if they hadn't been opened in years.

G. M. Muktibodh returned with the chai along with a little dish with simple snacks. He set down the tray on a makeshift coffee table, and sat down on his cushion. It was good, strong street chai, boiled like hell.

A silence hung over the room. Harshvarddhan didn't have the courage to begin the conversation. An ancient clock that probably needed a key to be wound stood against the wall in front of them. It was stopped. Next to it was a calendar with a drawing on its upper flap of Bal Gangadhar Tilak with his pagri turban wrapped around his head; the year on the calendar, Harshvarddhan noted, was 1964.

'I do realise that,' (the judge said after an endless sigh that had come from the very depths of his being) 'Mohandas is the real Mohandas.' His voice sounded as if it were coming from the bottom of a well; it was a quiet, peeping voice. He took a big sip of chai. The strain on his face loosened up a bit with the gulp and the taste of the hot drink.

'And that other man's a fraud. From start to finish, he's impersonating someone else. I know this, I know that his name is actually Bisnath, son of Nagendranath, and that he's stolen the identity of Mohandas and has been illegally living at A/11 Lenin Nagar working as deputy depot supervisor. He's a fraud, a crook, a sleaze!' he said, sometimes switching to English. Though he didn't speak loudly, there was a kind of sharp, steely resolve in his voice. He took a packet of bidis out of his pocket, picked one out, first blew on the fat end, lit it with a match and took a long, hard drag.

Harshvarddhan felt as if he'd been transported to another time and place.

'This is what I came here to tell you,' he said. 'But how do you know who is the real Mohandas?'

'It's not hard to figure out. If you're at all perceptive and have a little wits about you,' Muktibodh said, then began to look worried and got lost in thought. He took another long drag on the bidi. 'I've been up for three nights in a row, I can't sleep. This experience is absurd and very tense.' The bidi scissored between his fingers and was on the verge of going out. His gaze looked as if it were trained on himself.

'The system has collapsed, just like the twin towers. Now what's left for the subject of the state and the poor is anarchy and calamity. As far as I'm concerned, we are facing totally new forms of capital and power. Mohandas is being denied simple justice because it's something he can't buy. Oh!'

The veins of Muktibodh's forehead were throbbing and his hands were shaking. He seemed uneasy and stood up, and seeing that his bidi had gone out he took a pack of matches from his pocket and lit it up again.

'All ideas have their end. When intellectual and philosophical systems that at one time created a lot of change are transplanted into another, what happens is sometimes they can be transformed into totally hollow jargon, senseless bullshit, the ramblings of rogues. It's happened time and again throughout history. And yet...'

He puffed on his bidi and held the smoke in his lungs for a

long time. Maybe he wanted the nicotine to quiet the restlessness in his breathing. He began to cough. He pressed his left hand to his chest, and then said in a scratchy voice, 'But there's something in man, this strange thing, that no matter when, no matter what kind of power is trying to come down on him, it will never destroy him. And that thing's the quest for justice. The desire for justice is indestructible and timeless.'

He tossed the bidi he'd stuck between his index and middle fingers out the window. It had gone out.

Harshvarddhan Soni was confused. What kind of a person was this? To meet this kind of person disguised as a judge in this day and age seemed like an impossibility, a fantasy with a one-in-a-million chance of being real.

The judge was nervously pacing the room, but stopped suddenly – a bright, shining, mischievous twinkle now gleamed in his eyes that glowed like hot lead.

'It's OK, Harshvarddhan, don't feel like you need to stay, and please, don't worry. I know you haven't been able to sleep for the past few nights, just like me.' A huge smile spread over his face. 'Partner, you can sleep without worrying about a thing. Sleep like a dead horse. Now I've got to work on a little something.'

He approached Harshvarddhan and placed his hand on his shoulder; Harshvarddhan felt as if the hand had no weight at all. It was a hand made of paper, flowers, a dream, or language.

Gajanan Madhav Muktibodh, judge (first class), quietly whispered into Harshvarddhan's ear: 'There is one power that I have, one and only one power. That is... "secret judicial inquiry." I can myself make inquiries. Just leave it to me.'

When Harshvarddhan walked out of Muktibodh's flat it was

as if he was emerging from a cave of dreams and returning to his own time and reality: the one with Mohandas, Bisnath, himself, and the realities of today.

A short four days later, Viswanath and his father Nagendranath were arrested and sent to jail by order of G. M. Muktibodh, judge (first class), and, in accordance with sections 419, 420, 468, 467, and 403, were charged with counterfeiting, fraud, racketeering, theft, and embezzlement. The court ordered S. K. Singh, CEO of Oriental Coal Mines, to immediately begin official proceedings against Mohandas Vishwakarma, aka Vishwanath, deputy depot supervisor, and to report the findings of the proceedings to the court in two months' time. On top of this, proceedings and investigations should be launched in all concerned departments and divisions of the company against all managers and workers affiliated and connected with the matter either directly or indirectly. If the Oriental Coal Mines wanted to pursue the cases separately under criminal law, then this court would support such actions.

The news caused a huge stir. The arrest of the fake Mohandas was printed on page one of the newspapers. It sent ripples not just through the Oriental Coal Mines, but among officials and union leaders and workers in all sorts of factories and public sector enterprises. Several officials and workers were suspended. Others went on extended holiday. Everywhere there was panic and confusion. Thousands of Bisnath-like individuals had stolen the identities, qualifications, and abilities of others in desirable residential colonies like Lenin Nagar, Gandhi Nagar, Ambedkar Nagar, Jawahar Nagar, Shastri, Nehru, and Tilak Nagar – and had worked in their places for years, earning thousands of rupees with each pay cheque.

It turned out that Gajanan Madhav Muktibodh, judge (first class), Anuppur (M. P.) had invoked his emergency security power, and he himself had conducted a 'secret investigation' into the matter.

That night, he'd stayed up late reading. At nine in the morning he phoned his driver and instructed him to bring the government car that, up until then, he'd used only to drive to and from court. He made another call to H. S. Parasi (Harishankar Parasi), who was a public prosecutor, and a third call to S. B. Singh (Shamsher Bahadur Singh), who was the SSP of Anuppur. Each of the three officials set off to fulfill their respective duties with due diligence and faith. A fourth call he made to Harshvarddhan Soni.

'Partner, go get some notarised paper and be on standby!'

Shamshed Bahadur Singh recounted that the judge went straight to A/11 Lenin Nagar, near Matiyani crossing. Bisnath was out with Vijay Tiwari doing some favour for a politician. The only one at home was Kasturi, aka Reunkadevi, whose rackets were the chit fund, social services, kitty parties, and money games. The judge asked her right off the bat her father's and mother's names; Kasturi madam, aka Renukadevi, having seen the siren mounted atop the government car, got nervous.

The judge's vehicle then left Lenin Nagar and began heading back along the Mirzapur–Banaras road. Exactly thirty-five kilometres later the car turned onto the dirt road that went toward the village of Awazapur. Half an hour later, the car pulled up in front of quite a grand house in Lankapur village. The judge only had two questions for Lalu Prasad Pandey and his wife, Jai Lalita. Number one, their own names and the names of their children.

And the second, the names and addresses of their sons-in-law. Then he instructed public prosecutor H. S. Parsai to get the notarised paper from Harshvarddhan Soni and take their sworn statements.

The judge's car then arrived at the home of the head of the village panchayat, where he took his and other witnesses' testimony.

The SSP had a huge smile on his face. 'Fraudsters just can't think more than two steps ahead, and in the end, every last one of them gets caught. I called the SHO of Anuppur police station from Lankapur and told him to go to Bichiya Tola and Lenin Nagar to arrest Nagendranath and Bisnath, otherwise they would have escaped and caused lots of problems!'

The rest of the story is quite concise.

Harshvarddhan Soni and Mohandas were ecstatic with their victory. Kasturi danced and pirouetted throughout Purbanra. Once again Putlibai rummaged around the back of the rice bin until she found the bag of bisunbhog rice she'd stashed in there. The smell of the kheer being made with goat's milk, khandsari and bisunbhog filled every corner of the house. The myna bird used her tiny beak to help crack open the eggs in her nest, and the little chicks emerged, filling the rooms with their innocent chirping like a new kind of music.

The pain from Putlibai's rheumatism abated, and, for the first time in a long time, she swept the courtyard on her own. She sang with audible delight, but mixed in with the joyous bird-like voice was a sad note, too:

When you're not here
My world is lonely

No joy in gold or home,

In sun or moon

Harshvarddhan Soni told Mohandas that the next case he'd bring would be to get him his rightful job at the Oriental Coal Mines. *The court has confiscated all of your certificates, transcripts, and recommendations from Bisnath's service book. They'll be returned to you.* Mohandas embraced Harshvarddhan; his ravaged body was shaking, and he was getting choked up; tears of gratitude and joy flowed in equal measure, like a rain shower in the month of Shravan.

Biran Baiga hosted another all-nighter of feast and song and wine. Sitiya cooked a juicy pork dish made with mustard seed oil, garlic and onions, and garam masala. Three jugs of mahua were produced. This time, in addition to the dholak and manjira, Ram Karan brought a harmonium. Gopaldas, Biran, Bihari, Parmodi, and Mohandas all drank. Sitiya, Ramole, Kasturi, and Savitri also all took part in the libations. They sang and danced. Mohandas couldn't figure out how he managed to remember each song, one after the next; time simply came to a standstill.

This time Kasturi was the one who drank a little too much. Every few minutes she'd pull Mohandas over into her arms. 'Hu Hu Tu Tu! Wanna play kabbadi with me? Hu Hu Tu Tu!' she said each time, tickling Mohandas.

'Eh, scram, go back to Inspector Tiwari's cowshed!' Mohandas said, teasing her, and everybody thought this was the funniest thing.

Savitri chimed in. 'Hey, check out Tiwari! The police inspector's shit his underwear!' This set off a bomb of hysteria that echoed around Purbanra the rest of the night.

Mohandas and Biran Baiga stood up together in the middle of the courtyard as if they were in a courtroom. The questioning commenced.

Mohandas: 'You! What's your name? WHAT IS YOUR NAME? C'mon, tell the court, we don't have all day!'

Biran Baiga: 'My name is Biran Baiga. And my father's name is Dindua Baiga! Dindua Baiga!'

Mohandas: 'You! And What Is My Name? MY name? What IS it?'

Biran Baiga (driving his finger into his chest) 'You sonofa-bitch bum! Your name is Mohandas! MOHANDAS! Mohandas Kabirpanthi Bansor!'

Mohandas: 'And my father's name?'

Biran Baiga: 'You father's dead! His name was Kabadas.'

Mohandas: 'You! So if Mohandas is here, and my father Kabadas is up there, in heaven, then, Mr. Smartypants, who's the cuntworm sitting over there in jail in Anuppur?'

Birandas: (jumping up and down and clapping his hands) 'That's fryface depot supervisor Bisnath! Fraudster! And his father's a two-time fraudster. His wife? Fraudster! And the bigwigs in Lenin Nagar who run the coal mine? All fraudsters!'

Parmodi, Sitiya, Bihari, Ramkaran, Ramoli, Savitri, and Gopaldas's laughter rang anew as they picked up the tempo on the dholak, manjira, and harmonium.

(Don't you think that amid all the pain and sorrow and bleak colours of this story little drops of joy have been interspersed? Don't you think so? Well, you're right. In the rough reality of the lives of the poor and victims of injustice, sometimes little bright colours flash. Like when combined forces of power and capital suddenly swoop down in a surprise attach on the myna bird, utterly destroying her nest, and then all you can see are the feathers and drops of blood of the little chicks. These drops are never visible in the history book that's been written by the lackeys of a human resource minister of some political party. This is the job of a historian: to cover up the stains and spots at the edges of the clothing of his own time.)

The month was full of the unexpected. You won't find an account or news about what was happening 1050 kilometres from Delhi anywhere else outside this story. Here's a short summary of the circumstances that Mohandas's life passed through:

Gajanan Madhav Muktibodh, judge, first class, was all of a sudden transferred to Rajnandgaon, and he left Anuppur.

Ras Bihari Rai, Bisnath's lawyer, who was a well-known leader of the party in power and whose wife was a member of the city council, got both Bisnath and his father Nagendranath bailed out of prison with a single court hearing. Ras Bihari Rai was a skilled player of the politics of the day. As they were releasing Vishwanath aka Mohandas from prison after making bail, they cleverly wrote 'Mohandas' and nothing else into the Police Record. Because the final sentence had yet to be delivered, Mohandas aka Vishwanath was not a convinced criminal in the eyes of a law, but just a suspect. In other words, in the official police documents, the two men who were released on bail from the prison at Anuppur were let out under the names Mohandas (aka Vishwanath) and Kabadas (aka Nagendranath). The names that were written after this on the release orders were scribbled so they weren't legible.

And then all of a sudden one day the news came from Rajnandgaon that judge G. M. Muktibodh had had a brain haemorrhage and was taken in a coma to the Apollo Hospital in

Bilaspur. At the hospital, Congress party stalwart Srikant Verma, and his dear old friend, Nemichand Jain, were there with him. But after seventy-two hours of a tough fight between life and death, Gajanan Madhav Muktibodh, judge, first class, breathed his last breath. And with it he said, 'Hé Ram!'

With Harshvarddhan Soni, when he got the news of his death, was the inconsolable Mohandas Kabirpanthi Bansor of Purbanra village. With the judge's life had gone out his lone hope.

The most recent news is that Bisnath and his wife Renuka have been making a lot of money from their side businesses related to the coal mine. Bisnath and Vijay Tiwari are still in cahoots. These days he's openly come into politics and is running for a seat on the district council. And his caste brothers are also in positions of high power. They help him out in every way possible. He'll say, 'Who is the real Mohandas? Who is the fraud? That's something that I and I alone will decide! That two-bit piggy shithead cast aspersions on my honour, and took the job I had fair and square. So now I'll show him what true force is!'

When I went back to my village last week I saw that the look on Harshvarddhan's face was of numbness. His eyes were red. He said, 'I haven't slept the last three nights. I have no idea what I'm going to do. The people in Purbanra are telling the truth about Bisnath. The worst poisonous snake. A viper's viper.'

He let out a deep sigh. 'Every couple of days Bisnath creates some kind of catastrophic criminal act in Lenin Nagar. Sometimes he'll grab a gold chain off someone, or else he'll beat someone senseless. And when someone owes money to the chitfund his wife runs, she'll have them beat up, walk right into their house, and take whatever stuff she pleases. And then when a criminal complaint is lodged at the police station, it's done so in the name of Mohandas, since most of the people still know Bisnath as Mohandas. Then it's poor Mohandas, the real one, who gets arrested and dragged off by the Purbanra police.'

Harshvarddhan's eyes filled with tears of helplessness. 'Bisnath colluded with police inspector Vijary Tiwari and bought off the guards at the station with food and wine, and now they've beaten Mohandas within an inch of his life. They broke his hands and feet and he can't walk. And four days ago his mother Putlibai fell into a well and died. Kasturi is cobbling together whatever she can to put bread on the table.'

I looked up; Mohandas was approaching, limping heavily. He was not wearing the washed-out, patched up pants and torn checked shirt, but only a loin-cloth. His hair had fallen out, and he wore cheap round eyeglasses. He walked slowly, using a walking stick, shuffling along like an old man.

'Ram Ram, uncle!' he said upon seeing me, joining his palms together in greeting. The deep wrinkles on his face were a monument to his suffering and defeats. He looked like a very old man, maybe eighty or ninety. He sat down on the ground, using his walking stick as a support. But the gruff voice that came out of his mouth with a groan wasn't our local tongue, but Hindi, the 'national language.' He said:

'I take your hands and beg: please find a way to get me out of this. I am ready to go to any court and swear that I am not Mohandas. My father's name is not Kabadas, and he is not dead, he is alive. They really beat the hell out of me, the police did, on Bisnath's order. They broke my bones. It hurts to breathe it's so bad.'

I noticed his lips were cut badly and he was missing some teeth; they must have smashed them out in the police station. He could barely put two words together.

'Whoever wants to be Mohandas, let him be Mohandas. I am not Mohandas. I never did a BA. Didn't come out on top of my class. Never was fit for work. Just want to live in peace. Leave me be, no more beatings. If you want something, take it. Take what you need and fill up your homes. But leave me to my life and toil. Uncle, please stand by my side.'

It came out that Mohandas's eleven-year-old son Devdas hadn't been home in ten days. Some said that Bisnath had him disappeared, others said he'd fled to Mumbai in fright.

Still others claim to have seen him in the jungles of Bastar.

(It was the time when at the top of a hillside near Bharuch stood a thirty-year-old Dhanuhar archer named Raghav. Night after night he'd stay up late whittling down shaft after shaft of bamboo into arrows. He drew the bowstring taut and shot arrows at the sky, then ran down the hill to retrieve the arrows that'd come back down.

Again and again and again – countless times he fired arrows at the sky and retrieved them from the dirt.

But then the arrows began to be submerged under water, and it became difficult to find them and pull them out. The fields of the valleys that lay between the mountains were filling up with water: inundated, a massive flood. Village after village began to go under, and trees, too. North and south and east and west were going under; all memories were going under.

Yet thirty-year-old Raghav kept shooting arrows into the sky and running down to retrieve them as long as he himself wasn't swept under.

Where is Raghav now? Just where he was, where there's now nothing but water. A vast, bottomless sea where electricity is created. There once was a hilsa fish in Bharuch. The greatest fish in the rivers of India, the most magnificent in the world. The hilsa is only able to survive in the fast moving current of a river.

The hilsa at the dam is sick from the polluted water, and has probably died.

It happened at the same time as when I was writing this story in a language that imprisoned me inside just like Iraqis were imprisoned in Abu Ghraib. Or like Jews in 1943 were imprisoned inside a German gas chamber. Or like a drowned hilsa fish in dirty, stagnant, polluted waters. Or right now like Raghav Dhanuhar, still fighting.

This was the time of Mohandas, of you, of me, of Bisnath, of what we see this very day when we look outside our windows.

And the time everybody knows as the first decade of the twenty-first century, when all of us were celebrating the one hundred and twenty fifth anniversary of the birth of Premchand, the King of Hindi Fiction.

But really, tell the truth: Doesn't the name of Mohandas's village, Purbanra, remind you even a tiny bit of the Mahatma's Porbandar?

MANGOSIL

— This story is dedicated to Laghve,
Paul and Shailendra —

A PREFACE TO THE END OF TIME
(Reading this preface is mandatory)

This is the story of Chandrakant Thorat. It's also my story. And it's a story that takes place in the present day, in our own time, a tale with the sights and sounds of this day and age. A few of the characters have been cast out of their own space and time, and now stand in wait for the destruction at the end. I am one of them, living outside of my proper space and time, in a filthy quarter far from the finery and culture of the city. The efforts of human beings to lead lives in the shanty towns that circle the city on grabbed land eventually take shape, one unfortunate day, on the maps of a town planner, or property dealer, or urban coloniser. Then, the engineers of the empire of money send out the bulldozers – they fan out, non-stop – until even a dirty sprawl of shacks is transformed into a Metro Rail, a flyover, a shopping mall, a dam, a quarry, a factory, or a five-star-plus hotel. And when it happens, lives like Chandrakant Thorat's are gone for good.

⁓

Chandrakant Thorat is a friend of mine, and he's one of the characters of this story. My life is bound to his as if by decree or fate. Even if I didn't want it to be so, it would be.

You ought to know the truth: there are only two reasons lives like ours are stamped out. One: our lives are left over as proof of past and present sins and crimes against castes, races, cultures; they always want to keep this as hidden as they can. Two: our lives get in the way of the enterprising city, or act as a road bump in the master plan of a country that thinks of itself as a big player on the world stage. Our very humanity threatens to reveal the wicked culture of money and means as something suspect and unlovely. That's why whenever civilizations once developing, now on the brink of prosperity, decide to embark on a program of 'beautification', they try to root out such lives, the same way the mess on the floor is swept outside.

Suppose we fled these megalopolises to an exurb, or to the mountains, or into the forest, or to a small town? There, too, lives like ours would one day be inundated and swept away, just as the Harappan or Babylonian civilizations you must have read about in archeology books were also wiped out.

The memory of the destruction at the end of time lies in the psyche of every community of every people, including ours.

There is something else you should know. Whenever our lives are steamrolled in the name of cultural progress and cultural beauty to profit the rich city or state; or when lives drown for power and energy: it's not just us. The deer, butterflies, birds, elephants, pipal and teak trees, the flora (divine beings all) are also washed away from this earth. Beings that descended from heaven, thousands of years ago, in the ancient treta or dwapar epochs; beings that settled into rocks and books so that our suffering might be eased. To allow us to endure our pain and desolation. To light our way like a candle or firefly or light bulb in the darkness. When violence permeates everything, and reality has become a nightmare, these creatures carry us into a dream.

You know the truth: none of it is meant for us. Not the medicine of rich, developed nations that give relief from suffering, or the energy that creates the illusion of light and wind and words and dazzle – none is meant for us. Top-tier hospitals, banks, institutions, parliaments, courts, airports, and wide boulevards aren't for us. We're chased away from these places, or crushed underfoot.

Only they may inhabit the buildings and institutions built by civilizations of wealth. Their constitutions only serve to protect their interests. Their language of poetry and legend is covered with our blood, sweat, sorrow, and tears.

Their poems and epics aren't ours. They want to keep us out of everything: poetry, prose, music, cities, work, industry, the marketplace. We're the drudging, untouchable, poor, unemployed, dissatisfied, anxious, and hungry people who, to them, are utterly unknown. They despise us each and every moment; each and every moment, they wish to do away with us.

What do you think? In 2003, could what's happened in Afghanistan, Iraq, Bosnia, or what happened in the middle of the twentieth century in Hiroshima-Nagasaki, Korea-Vietnam, or what happened two-and a half thousand years before Christ in Mohanjodaro, Harappa or Mesopotamia, or what's happening right now, as I'm writing these lines, in Karbala, Baghdad, Fallujah, Najaf, Nasiriyah or in the Gaza strip – is it so different from what's happening in Delhi's Gurgaon, Noida, Silampur, Bhilasava, Rohini, Jiyasaray, Mahrauli? Or different from what's happening on the banks and shores of the rivers Narmada, Son, Betava, Krishna-Cauveri, Dajla, Yangtzee, Amazon, Volga, Mississisppi, Jambeji, Thames, Nil, Sindhu, Ganga, Tungbhadra, and Kosi?

Read this preface to the end of time very carefully! Pore over each and every word and sentence, sift through the blank spaces and the silences in between. Close your eyes, focus all your concentration on our time, our age, and take a deep breath, a very deep breath. Breathe in the sun, the radiant, fiery ball that's fixed in the sky. Take it all into your lungs: after all, the sun's the only thing that connects us into harmony with time and space. Lie down on your back and relax. Forget the here and now and ponder the immortal Lord of Time, Shiva. The present moment is ephemeral, a mirage. Now place your right thumb between your two eyebrows and place your index finger on your forehead. Yes, good! Very good! Remain still, very still. And as soon as you do this – pop! – a little burst rushes forth, and the mystery of all life and creation and the universe will appear in front of you in the dim light of your own consciousness.

And after being liberated by your deep encounter with time, you too, like Chankrakant Thorat and me, will begin to wait for the great flood, the inescapable and omnivorous fire.

To anticipate the apocalypse.

To await Armageddon.

To hold on for a great new revolution, the likes of which has never been seen before.

The massive destruction that's essential for anything new to rise up.

The mad volley of an age, of which a new epoch is born. A new civilization comes into existence. After the present fades into oblivion, everything can begin anew. A revolutionary moment marking the end of now and the beginning of to be.

Ah! And on that day, on a tiny, green leaf of a pipal or banyan or wishing tree, swims a little baby, screaming and swimming on top of the gigantic waves in a vast, fearsome ocean that's swallowing all the earth and all creation into its belly. The sound of the baby's weeping and wailing echoes throughout the whole universe.

Waaaah! Waaaah!

On a primitive wooden boat, without rudder or paddle... atop the churning tide, silently floating... flickering in the distance.

Ah! That wooden boat is very old... slowly floating off into the distance...

Oh, yes, I forgot to tell you something about Chandrakant and me... it's that our head – yes, the round head that every living man has on his shoulders – it's become big, and is continuously getting bigger. Doctors say it's an incurable disease...

And the disease is called – 'Mangosil.'

And it's a disease for which medical scientists know no cure. Neither allopathic doctors, homoeopathic doctors, nor ayurvedic doctors. And nothing in Baba Ramdev's *Yoga and Pranayama Breathing Exercises to Tackle All Diseases*. It's true, an old fakir (you can find him at the shrine of Amir Khusrau, 'the other master') once said that there is a book in which its cure does indeed exist. But with a heavy sigh, he added that the problem was that this book is yet to be written.

For the past several years, both Chandrakant Thorat and I have carried the burden of our big heads on our shoulders, ever in search of that book. The fakir, whose eyes were red like the eyes of fire ants, creatures the creator did not give the capacity for sleep, animals that do not slumber once in their entire lives, insects that continuously carry thirty times their own body weight, or more; this fakir said, 'A curse of rain and ruin on those who pen books of wickedness by their own hand and claim it the writ of Allah. And on those who claim that these books will bring an end to the sorrows and trials of man. Ruin will come to those who write these books, and ruin will befall those who profit from them.'

The fakir added, as he was leaving, 'Look at your own life, and at the lives all around you. One day, on your own, you will stumble upon that book. But remember this: in it, you will find fire and water. And you will find a leaf or a boat above the tip of a flame, or the top of a wave, somehow swimming, somehow surviving. And you will hear a voice – a voice that will give birth to all other voices in the world that comes after.'

Chandrakant and I, carrying the burden of our heavy heads of bottomless sorrow on our shoulders, have been in constant search for that book.

You can see for yourselves: our eyes are red like the eyes of fire ants. We aren't blessed with the capacity to sleep, and, in our life, we're carrying thirty times our own weight. Are you watching? Can you see the blood that pours forth beyond the bounds of our speech? The same words that bring nothing but punishment without pause! Time and again, we're forced to leave town. Place after place, they're kicking us out.

Words that, one day, will give rise to all the world's languages. Because the old fakir with eyes as red as a fire ant, sitting that day in front of the minor court of Hazarat Nizzumaddin – the shrine of Amir Khusrau, the first poet of the language we now call Hindi, said so.

Jahangirpuri bylane number seven

Buttressed by what is said to be the largest fruit and vegetable market in Asia lies a neighbourhood in Northwest Delhi – Jahangirpuri. If you're travelling between India and Pakistan on the *Goodwill Bus*, you'll see what looks like a residential area right before the bypass road on the left hand side – rising up from the mud and the muck, that's Jahangirpuri. But from a distance the land between the highway and the settlement doesn't seem to be made of simple blackened ooze, dirt and water, but instead from a chemical mix consisting of a molten solution of motor oil, grease, gasoline, and plastic. Might as well throw in the rotting organic matter from the fruit and vegetables as well.

Jagangirpuri was most assuredly settled without a planning map. Over many years, people showed up, built a house wherever they found some space, and settled down. In the surrounding area you'll find what looks like ancient ruins, giving the impression that this area has been gradually inhabited over a period of centuries. If you're flying overhead and glance down, you'll see a mishmash of half-built houses. It's as if someone took the waste material from wealthy Delhi's architectural finest, and swept it clean out here into a pile: a trash heap of higgeldy-piggeldy brick houses tossed in the middle of a black chemical slime bog that exudes the stench of rotting fruit and vegetables. There are exceptions – a few multi-storied, modern houses. But this is like what Delhi, Bangalore, Hyderabad, and Bombay look like from way up in the sky compared to the rest of India: incongruous tokens of priceless, shining marble stuck in the mire and mud of the subcontinent's swamp of chilling poverty.

Narrow alleys or bylanes, no more than ten to twelve feet wide, wind through the rows of houses that are built right on top of one another in Jahangirpuri. In some places, they are as narrow as eight to ten feet from one side to the other. You can traverse these bylanes, without fear of collision, only on foot or by cycle. During the hot season, people bring their cots outside and sleep; settlements like these are the hardest hit by the capital city's frequent power and water cuts. Gossip, STDs, dengue fever, black magic, criminality, and disease spread most vigorously in places like Jahangirpuri. This summer, the channels built for water drainage were all running open, and every morning, the young and the old and infirm squatted above them and did their business. The smell rising from the ditches after the water is turned off gives the neighbourhood its unmistakable stamp.

It's half past ten at night right now in bylane number seven, where a fat, dark-complexioned man of forty-five or fifty tiptoes down the alley loosely clasping a bag in his right hand. It's dark; all five lampposts in the streets are without bulbs. The bright light shining in the eyes of the people sleeping outside bothered them, so they unscrewed the bulbs. At the end of the bylane was (until just a few months ago) a working light, but Gurpreet and Somu from bylane three broke it because they were running around with Deepti and Shalini from E-7/2 of bylane seven, and liked it dark when they brought the girls back late at night on the back of their Hero Honda motorbikes. Deepti and Shalini were C-list models; aside from appearing in cheap ads for underwear and hair removal products, they were also available at nights in five-star hotels, or for private parties. An older lady of the night lived in house E-6/3. Her husband had been run over by a bus in front of the Liberty Cinema three years before. Since then, she has been supporting her three kids and elderly mother-in-law with the help of the kind-hearted men who visit her after hours. She has full sympathy from the residents of bylane seven, and even if the bulb at the far end hadn't been removed, no one would have batted an eye.

The man with the bag in his hand walks ten steps down the darkness of bylane seven and, halting in front of the ditch, removes a pint bottle of Bonnie Scot, and downs it in one go, before tossing away the empty bottle and pissing in the ditch. The man is Chandrakant Thorat.

Even though he was middle-aged, Chandrakant enjoyed new Indy Pop like *'Jhanjar wali hoke matvali'* and *'Channave ghar aa jaave.'* It was funny that the favourite music of Chandrakant, who spoke pidgin Marathi and just passable Hindi, was Panjabi pop music. And whenever love stirred in his heart for Shobha, his wife, the emotion found expression in Panjabi: *Baby, baby, what can I do? My heart's horn honks when I see your pretty face! You oughta hear it, baby! You gotta hear it, baby!* Shobha responded, chiding him, 'Coming home drunk again? How many times have I told you, drink as much as you'd like, but do it at home. If anything ever happened to you, I'd end up like our lady of the night! Then what?'

143

These words sobered him up instantly. He certainly didn't want to die and force his wife to rely on kind-hearted men.

'You just doused my Bonnie Scot with bitter herbs. Make me some food. I've got to go to work early tomorrow.' Then Chandrakant was silent. He hung his head low as he ate, stretched and yawned, then lay down to sleep on the mat on the floor. She ate afterwards, then did household chores late into the night, washing dishes, chopping vegetables for the morning, ironing Chandrakant's pants and shirt, until finally, at midnight, she sat by the outdoor tap and bathed. By the time she finished her work, humming some old song while she adjusted the fan on top of the trunk, Chandrakant was already snoring.

RUNNING OFF WITH SHOBHA

Shobha and Chandrakant had been living together for some thirty years. Chandrakant had fled with her from Sarani where she had been living with her husband, Ramakant.

Ramakant had no job and no skills: he ran around wherever he could to try and get a small piece of the action. He was addicted to playing the market, and also worked part-time for the police as a false witness. Those days, the eyes of a certain police inspector had fallen on Shobha; every night, the inspector came over to their house to drink and eat. Every night for three months, the middle-aged inspector's lust fell on Shobha. Those three tortuous months in Shobha's life were worse than hell. He arrived at the house around nine at night; as soon as he stepped in the door he took off his uniform and hung it on a peg. Now down to his sweaty, smelly, dirty undershirt and brown, greasy

shorts, he took a seat on the little mat on the floor, and forbade
the outside door to be closed because then there would be no
breeze to cool him down. Ramakant served the inspector as
if he were his butler, running back and forth to the kitchen
and market for salty namkeen snacks, hard-boiled eggs, and,
whenever the need arose, another bottle of hooch. Ramakant
also kept his glass nearby, so whenever he had a free moment
after running around fetching things for the inspector, he sat
down next to the inspector and joined him for a shot. He
was proud of those moments; they were a real honour and
treat. He laughed and joked with the inspector, and chided
his wife Shobha – 'Hurry up, squeeze the lemon, bring the
snacks! Inspector sahib likes green chilies. Thinly, cut them
thinly!' Or, 'Don't just toss the dish on the floor! Place it in
the man's hand, nicely, gently, that's it. And what happened
to the coriander? Didn't I just buy two bunches for inspector
sahib to enjoy?'

'Ramakant, how about one more?' the inspector said.
'And give your better half something to drink, too. Tomorrow
a friend of mine is coming. We'll have a party!' the inspector
said.

Ramakant's face lit up at the mention of a party. A party
meant he would get to eat mutton or chicken, with plenty of
snacks, too, plus more good booze. On top of that, he was
always able to ferret away a few rupees from the money the
inspector gave him for the food and drink.

'Consider it done, sahib! So will it be mutton or chicken?
Should I have her make fish or pakoras to go with the drinks?
She's a fantastic cook. How much meat, four pounds or five?
And how much whisky d'you think'll be necessary?' He grinned

shamelessly and added, 'See, if there's any food left over it'll be a big help the next day. After a big party Shobha's in no shape at all until two or three in the afternoon.'

After getting drunk, the inspector might launch into song, or start hurling vile curses. He had convinced himself that Shobha was thrilled to have found such a robust specimen of a man as he, and one with money, too – particularly after playing long-suffering wife to the penniless, shiftless, good-for-nothing Ramakant. The inspector also came to accept that in her heart of hearts, Shobha fancied him indeed. And once the inspector understood this, he stepped up his abuse of Ramakant, chastising and reprimanding him at every word, pausing to fasten his gaze on Shobha, to whom he started sweet-talking. It transpired that since she was little she had a soft spot for dark gulab jamun, not to mention her other favourite sweet: rabri-ilichi kulfi. How was this loser going to procure such sweetmeats for Shobha? The inspector at once sent Ramakant out to fetch the delicacies. As soon as he was out the door, the inspector drew her near.

His hairy potbelly poked out from a filthy, stinking undershirt, underneath which he grabbed Shobha's head and brought it to his sweaty, soiled crotch. Her every breath caught a second stench of the raw sewage rivulets that crisscrossed the neighbourhood. She nearly retched on the spot. The inspector stroked her hair as he swigged from the bottle. Sounds issued from her mouth as if she were getting the sour taste of a lemon and the hot part of a chili both at once. The door to the outside was left open, a fact that late-night passers-by often noticed. Moreover, the little vacant patch of land in front of the house was a popular spot for people to stop and answer the call of nature. Here, in perfect darkness, a crush of young nogoodniks, out for a midnight stroll, gathered by the house of police flunky Ramakant to watch live porn.

'Party night' meant that the inspector brought a buddy. Those nights, Shobha endured inhuman torment and suffering. After getting well drunk, the men let loose the beast within. And in that room, Shobha fell victim to the violence of the wild animals and the frenzy they unleashed. Once they got going, they sang, drank more, praised the fish pakoras to high heaven, laughed and giggled, groped and fondled Shobha, squeezed and pinched. Ramakant encouraged them in all this.

A fat and flabby fair-skinned contractor was brought to one such party by the inspector. He was in his late fifties, early sixties. That night they had even set up a VCR to watch porn; back then, VCRs had just come out and could be rented in the bazaar. Leering at the stunning Shobha, he casually let slip that this year he was going to be elected as municipal councillor, having locked up all the votes from this neighbourhood and the surrounding ones.

That night Shobha was taken to the gates of hell. The contractor and inspector committed unnatural acts, including the contractor inserting a beer bottle in her rectum. The inspector laughed, 'What the heck are you doing!?'

'What am I doing?' The contractor overflowed with delight. 'Just a little drilling from the back side to bore a big hole so that the motor'll hum from the under side! I've got a twenty-horsepower tractor!' Shobha gasped for breath, blood dripping on the rug and floor, while porn flashed on the TV. Unconsciousness relieved her from the torments. It was nearly four in the morning when the inspector and contractor finally made their way home. Shobha was greeted with splitting pain when she came to; she wanted to get up and get dressed and wash off the blood and semen. She found Ramakant mounting her. She gave him a kick. Then, in fits and groans, she found the bucket of water kept just outside the front door and began washing herself, not a stitch of clothing covering her body.

As she sat groaning and washing off her blood and the spit and semen of the contractor, inspector, and Ramakant, she had the feeling that at four in the morning she had been ogled by the eyes of many men in the darkness from across the bylane. Bloodletting, blood-soaked, bestial violence: these people stayed up all night to watch this? Not a wink of sleep, smelling the shit from the sewage all night long? This was their idea of fun?

Almost a week later, the contractor showed up one afternoon in his car. The inspector was with him. They brought all sorts of goodies for Shobha: saris with matching tops, lingerie, teddies, lace panties, salwar-kurta, bangles, jewellery, and more. The contractor seemed very pleased and, between sips of chai, informed her that he had appointed her Director of the All-Women's Welfare Association, meaning that now he would take her with him on tour to Mumbai, Nagpur, Pune, Kolhapur, and other cities.

That day, Chandrakant, a servant in the contractor's employ, was introduced to Shobha.

Six weeks later, at a government rest house in Jalgaon, the contractor took her to the VIP room. There, party underway, Shobha slipped out under the pretext of needing to change her clothes and, bag packed with everything she had, ran off with Chandrakant to Delhi, where they rented a ground floor flat for five hundred rupees a month at house number E-3/1, bylane number seven, Jahangirpuri. He found part-time work as a helper at a department store in Vijaynagar and she began making food and snacks and pickle and preserves for neighbouring households.

Fleeing from Jalgaon with Chandrakant that night had rescued Shobha from a terrible crime; Chandrakant had masterminded the escape. Fifteen days had passed since the last party, when the contractor had announced they were going to Jalgaon. He had been busy with some construction project. Only the inspector had come in the meantime, two or three times. Shobha waited quietly for the next party, for which she had purchased thirteen rupees worth of rat poison kept hidden in her secret bundle. She mixed it into the goatmeat dish, and was ready to serve it to the inspector, contractor, and her husband, Ramakant. After she did, Shobha faced a dilemma: eat it and herself perish, or don't eat it and run off with Chandrakant? She kept her plan hidden from Chandrakant; he seemed so guileless and honest that she was sure he would never allow her to go through with it. Chandrakant finally acceded to them running away together from Jalgaon, though he was clearly scared.

Shobhba in the half flat

E-3/1 was a four-story house. There was space underneath the stairs that, with a little imagination, formed something like a room. Ten feet long, seven feet wide, not exactly a room, but a half flat, and thus with no proper front door. Chandrakant and Shobha fastened two planks of wood over the opening. The first they nailed to the top with scrap metal and hung a blue plastic curtain. The second served as a sliding door leaf. On cold winter days when both Chandrakant and Shobha went out, they kept the door closed. In front of the door, or wall, or board, or whatever you want to call it, was an additional space that measured about four-and-a-half feet. On the left side was a little tap where Shobha and Chandrakant did all their bathing, laundry, and dishes. They called it 'the balcony'; two feet below was an open sewer. A strong, sour smell continuously wafted upwards along with a buzzing swarm of flies. A few days ago Chandrakant had found another board to cover it up.

They slept on a coarse little mat spread on the floor of their half flat, which they called, in English, the 'room.' Chandrakant and Shobha also owned a banged-up tin trunk in which they kept items used infrequently. Also kept in the trunk were the bangles, jewellery, saris, and salwars from the inspector and contractor; stainless steel and glass pots and plates from her parents when she got married; a pair of silver anklets; her mangalsutra wedding thread; a toe ring; armlet; a sari of silver thread. A half-inch strip of plywood was fastened above the trunk, on top of which perched the household's most valuable and necessary item, a fan. It was because of the fan they were able to sleep in the heat, without harassment from flies and mosquitoes. When it went on the blink, the despondent pair would go out to fetch the electrician and wouldn't rest until he'd fixed it. But it rarely stopped working. Flip the switch and it purred to life with a loud whoosh. The strong flow of cool air made Chandrakant and Shobha very happy.

In the corner of the room was a little stove that ran on wood scraps. That's where Shobha cooked, and no food was more delicious than Shobha's. He had been hooked on Shobha's cooking since the days of Sarni when he went in the big car to the parties at Ramakant's with his boss, the contractor. He used to pull right up to the door, making it a little difficult for the passersby who liked to peer inside the house. The contractor would turn up the tape deck as loud as it would go, drowning out both the noise of the 'party' and the shrieks of Shobha. Chandrakant was right there, stretched out in the back of the car, listening to the music issuing from its sound system. He had no idea what was going on inside. He never even peeked.

His eyes opened to find Shobha banging on the car window. She brought him food, a thali with roti, meat curry, onions, and more, sometimes a bit of rice. He liked her meat curry so much that it seemed there was never enough. This happened two or three times; Shobha began to sense his fondness, maybe because the two were around the same age. This was thirty years ago, when Shobha was nineteen or twenty, and villagers didn't pay attention to age differences between bride and groom. Ramakant was between thirty and thirty-five. The inspector who those days raped Shobha daily couldn't have been younger than forty-five, and the contractor, boss of servant Chandrakant, must have been nearing sixty.

Chandrakant, a young man of nineteen, was utterly different from these middle-aged, savage, stinking men; he stretched out in the back of the car, eyes closed, quietly listening to music, never asking for seconds, never taking a peek inside the house to see what went on during the 'party.'

That night she quietly crept to the car door window and, peering inside, saw Chandrakant mopping up the last of meat sauce with a roti, two more still on his thali.

'Do you want some more meat and sauce?' she asked, startling Chandrakant.

'No, no, this is plenty!'

Shobha met his reply with a smile. 'Then what's the use of the other roti?'

Chandrakant didn't have an answer.

She brought another katori dish full of meat and sauce, and two more roti as well. It pleased her as Chandrakant silently took the bread and lowered his head to begin eating. She watched him as he ate. He suddenly lifted up his head: his hair was a mess, his mouth full of food. He stared at Shobha and blushed as he broke into a kind of giggle.

It was like the end of a lifesaving rope that dangled in front of the black hole of her hellish life. She decided to grab it and run away, not knowing whether it was out of love or from an intense desire to be free.

The next party, Shobha informed the inspector, contractor, and Ramakant, who were busy eating fish pakoras and drinking, that she was going outside to serve Chandrakant his food. Once there, she got in the car and told him everything. She showed him her legs, back, chest, and neck for him to examine. 'Someone might come, I can't show you the rest here,' Shobha began. 'But mark my words, one day I'll be dead and they'll throw my body away. Save me however you can. Take me anywhere. I'll do your laundry, clean and dust, cook for you every day, wash the dishes. You like my meat curry, right? I can cook better. I can put a masala into the dish that'll fill the whole house with the most unbelievable fragrance you've ever smelled. If you want me to sleep outside, in the courtyard, on the stoop, I will. I don't need sheets or blankets. I can live with the clothes on my back. When you're not making money, I'll make it for you.'

The tape deck was still blaring music; twenty-year-old

Shobha hiccupped between her little sobs. 'You can do to me what the inspector and builder do to me and I won't say a word. If it hurts, I won't cry, I won't scream. I'll stop the blood, I won't allow myself to bleed. I'll clean everything up without a fuss, no one will know. I'll just keep smiling. You can tear me to bits and I'll keep smiling. I'll stay by your side and serve your every need. I'll nurse you when you get sick, soothe your body with massage. Do with me whatever you want, your heart's desire – I won't stop you. If you bring someone else I'll serve her too. Just get me out of this trap.' Shobha had gripped Chandrakant's shirtsleeve as if she would never let go, as if it were a root on a riverbank she suddenly found, and clung to, like life itself, in spite of being swept under by the current.

Listening to twenty-year-old Shobha, nineteen-year-old Chandrakant felt for the first time he wasn't just a servant in the contractor's employ. He could be more, and this thought gave rise to a kind of self-confidence he'd never had. Just then, Ramakant appeared. He saw Shobha attached to Chandrakant's sleeve, sitting close in the back seat of the car, telling him things, crying. In one fell swoop he opened the door, seized Shobha, and dragged her out. 'Did you come out here to feed him or fuck him, you whore. Haven't had enough yet?'

This was that same violent night when the contractor shredded Shobha's rectum with a beer bottle and she passed out from the bleeding. That night was also the first time Chandrakant heard her scream. A scream that carried so much pain it pierced the closed car window and even Chandrakant's eardrum. He panicked, sat up, and switched off the music. And for the first time he rolled down the window and stuck his head outside.

Inside, they had switched off the light; all there was to see was shifting shadows in the dark. He listened, but the only thing he could make out was the fearsome growling of wild animals issuing from inside the house, and it sounded as if they had found their prey and were tearing it to bits in a frenzy. For the first time, he despaired of Shobha's fate, she who had just a few minutes ago clung to his shirtsleeve, whose tears still moistened the same sleeve, whose curry and roti he had just finished eating. The image of her tearful face flashed before his eyes, and he felt as if she were still there with him. Chandrakant thought, I will absolutely help her out of that trap and lift her out of the pit.

Fear, however, reared its head inside of nineteen-year-old Chandrakant. The inspector and contractor were very powerful. He had seen their acts of barbarity with his own eyes. He knew from conversations with them and by the way they talked about places like Lucknow, Bhopal, Bombay, Delhi, and Calcutta that their influence stretched far and wide. They could get to wherever they wanted to go. And they would get to wherever he took this girl: the inspector, the contractor, their flunkeys – they would find them, there was nowhere to hide.

Chandrakant was in a tangle of fear and nerves and worry. That's why when he fled the house in Jalgaon with Shobha, he had wrapped a towel around his face and covered his body with a sheet. Shobha, however, beamed non-stop with a joy that bordered on rapture. As the train left Sarani station with the two safely inside their compartment, Shobha stowed her trunk and bundle and Chandrakant's bag underneath the berth with such delicacy and care it was as if she would make her new home right there on the train with Chandrakant – as if she was going to light a little cooking stove on the floor of the train and start a household. The carriage in which the two passengers rode rumbling along the iron rails wasn't made of wood, glass, and steel, but was transformed into a simple courtyard of fragrant adobe, where sweet spicy smells mixed with the rising smoke of the cooking stove, where a twenty-year-old girl, leisurely humming a song, rolled out the roti, fully absorbed in her work.

Something in this was quite pleasing to Chandrakant; time and again he wanted to break into song. What that pleasing something was, however, he wasn't able to fully comprehend.

The nest and eggs of a bird

Ah ha! So this is what had been so pleasing to Chandrakant that day on the moving train, the thing he wasn't able to fully understand.

It was some ten days after they found the half flat in the Jahangirpuri neighbourhood of Delhi at E-3/1, lane seven. The two of them had spent the first few days purchasing household goods for their mini-place, cleaning and setting up house. Chandrakant had found work as a shop assistant in a department store in Vijaynagar, which is also known as Kingsway Camp. Vijaynagar was no more than six kilometres from Jahangirpuri, with plenty of buses at the Aazadpur bus stand headed that way. He set off for work at six in the morning, came back at two in the afternoon for lunch, and returned to work at three thirty. It was nearly nine at night by the time he came back for good. Shobha had no idea how much money she had run off with from Sarani – it had easily covered the stove, fan, curtains, tarp, tin trunk, sheets and blankets, cup and saucer sets, pressure

155

cooker, thali dishes, glasses, food staples, tea and sugar, and all other household necessities. Smiling, she plunged her hand into her rainbow flower vinyl purse (a treasure-chest as bountiful as Tutankhamen's), and withdrew as much money as she pleased.

Day three after their arrival in Delhi Shobha began calling Chandakant 'Chandu' while he continued calling Shobha Shobha. Chandrakant began to get a little worried watching Shobha buy so much stuff, but she just scooped her hand into the flowered purse and said, 'Don't worry, Chandu! No worries at all! I hit the big one with Ramakant and inspector and contractor's cash.'

It was a Monday, when the bazaar at Vijaynagar was closed and Chandrakant had the day off.

He stretched out on the ground in the little room and began listening to the radio. *Oh don't shake down the apples from my tree! A little thorn will break the skin in a flash!* Every once in awhile he joined in. As he sang along, Shobha's voice rang in from outside, 'Nice voice, Chandu, it's like you're Kishore Kumar singing along with Lata Mangeshkar! Today's a singing kind of day!'

Chandrakant gazed outside, transfixed. Shobha was sitting next to the tap on the 'balcony' bathing, rubbing the soles of her feet with a little pumice stone, her sari bunched up to her thighs. As she poured water over her head with the red plastic mug, it was as if her sari was dissolving in the water, the sari turning to liquid and washing over her skin in glistening colours, clinging tightly to her body, revealing more and more of her wet form.

Chandrakant felt a lump in his throat, his voice began to crack, and so he stopped singing along with the radio and started staring at Shobha. His gaze must have burned into her backside; she turned around suddenly. 'What happened, Mr. Mohammed Rafi crooner man?' she teased. 'Lose your voice? Cat got your tongue, Chandu? Feeling shy?'

He didn't say a word, but just kept staring. Lather ran down her face, little white soap bubbles popped on her closed eyelids, she couldn't see a thing. This was the first time Chandrakant could observe her the way he wanted for as long as he wanted to. Beneath the folds of her sari, she lathered her chest, bar of soap in hand.

Chandrakant realised for the first time how huge her eyes were, just like the actress Hema Malini's, but bigger, even bigger.

They had been living together in the half flat for ten days, and he had known her even longer, from before, in Sarani, but he had never really looked at her body and her eyes as he did now. Chandrakant felt embarrassed for having spent so much time with Shobha – for having lived so long – without ever having been as close as he was now to the kind of body and shape of eyes that this girl had.

And how this girl looked though the soap lather that glittered like dewdrops, how it took his breath away, this was a new sensation.

Shobha stood up in her dripping wet sari and began drying her hair with a towel.

The magnetic field that originated from the water tap and enveloped him was also something new. It was like a zap from inside inducing him toward her with full force. His mind was in a bad way. He could see only colours swimming in front of his eyes, like the soap bubbles that floated in the air.

He walked up behind Shobha and clasped her around the

waist, then lifted her back into the half flat, the ten-by-seven 'room' that, for the moment, was the Delhi home of these two winged creatures.

Shobha said nothing. She was still wet; her hair too, eyes closed, face flushed with a flame that slowly let its heat seep over her body, and into her blood, until heat rose from her skin and met Chandrakant's lips. Not a drop of dew escaped his waiting mouth while hands explored every place on Shobha's body, tracing her wet skin.

The little mat on the floor beside the trunk, in the cramped half flat, was wringing wet. And atop that wet rug Chandu and Shobha seized one another as if at the epicentre of a consuming blaze. Soap bubbles of all hues seeped through the room, while outside on the balcony it wasn't water that gushed from the tap and noisily filled the bucket, but a rainbow of colour.

Shobha felt as if she was sinking into a deep dream on a magic carpet, not just lying on a rug. Her wet sari lay to the side, while atop her body was a blushing nineteen-year-old boy, smiling nervously, rather than the old, savage inspector, or contractor, or the husband she had been made to marry. That night in Sarani, she had grabbed hold of the edge of the rope that sprang from the smile of the boy born while eating her homemade curry and roti. And now it looked as if she might make it out alive.

It was as if the mouth of nineteen-year-old Chandrakant, whom she had begun to call Chandu, was still stuffed with the bits of her food, hungry and blushing as he smiled. Overcome with love for Shobha, he gathered her tangled hair in his hands and kissed her feverishly.

After that Monday, some thirty years ago, and a mere ten

days after the two of them had moved to their half flat at E-3/1, bylane number seven, Jahangirpuri, Shobha had begun referring to the covering on the floor as the carpet rather than a rug. She hummed while she worked, and after Chandrakant left for work in Vijaynagar, she sang duets with Lata Mangeshkar and Asha Bhosle on the radio.

Shobha prepared food for the two of them, peeled and chopped and sliced the vegetables, did their laundry, took naps, while Chandrakant swept her up and onto the magic carpet where the two of them would make love in a blaze of heat. Like this, years passed, Shobha grew plump, Chandrakant's hair thinned and turned grey, both of them sometimes fell ill, then got better, all the while and for thirty years playing the nonstop game of fanning the flames atop their magic carpet.

Shobha got pregnant seven times. She registered with the government hospital in Aadarsh Nagar, stitched and sewed clothes and booties and a bed for the baby, and ate and drank with great precaution. But either she miscarried, or the baby succumbed to an illness a few months after birth – each and every time. Chandrakant and Shobha were devastated. They decided that the mosquitoes and bacteria from the sewage gutter in front of their house had infected the babies with some illness; a thick, damp, and often strong stench came through their windows from the gutter. During the monsoon season, earthworms, centipedes, millipedes, snails, and frogs would crawl or hop from the gutter into their flat. One time when Shobha and Chandrakant were deep in the middle of playing their favourite game on the magic carpet, Shobha screamed when she saw a baby snake slithering on the ground off to her left. Another time it was a boa constrictor that sprang out from behind a box. Things got even worst during the rainy season – spiders were everywhere.

Both of them wished to move somewhere else, somewhere clean and tidy. But as time went on, rents began to soar. Chandrakant had always been on the lookout for another job or additional income, but nothing ever materialised. His boss at the shop, Gulshan Arora, was a good man, and no other shopkeeper would have paid a better salary. Over the thirty years, Arora had become an elderly seventy-year-old. Both his daughters had been married off, and he had one son who ran a small travel agency in Paharganj. Father and son didn't get along, and the son didn't care about the father's shop. The son, too, was already married, and had for the past several years waited for his father to die so he could sell the Kwality Departmental Stores. Gulshan Arora seemed to have an inkling of his son's wishes: time and again after a serious illness he returned from the brink of death, as if to dash his son's hopes. Gulshan Arora placed great faith in Chandrakant, since he didn't have any other option. The store limped along, but Arora still had to pay expenses.

Gulshan Arora was by then totally alone; his wife had died a dozen or so years ago. He had detained Chandrakant at his house on several occasions for late-night rum-drinking and chicken-eating sessions. He told Chandrakant not to worry about his inevitable death: he had left the store to his younger daughter, and had made a provision in his will for Chandrakant to the amount of 200,000 rupees. After the third or fourth drink, Gulshan Arora got animated and waxed philosophical. Chandrakant was aware that his boss, in spite of his age, brought home call girls, and was continuously taking herbal supplements and vitamin boosters called 'Lion Life,' 'Shot Gun,' and 'Hard Rock Candy Man' – these were the days before anyone had heard of Viagra or 40-60 Plus.

Chandrakant, while listening to his seventy-year-old boss's elaborate stories, would often begin to long for the man's death – and just then, Gulshan Arora by some means sensed his thoughts, smiled from ear to ear, and said, 'Chandu! Enough with your dreaming of my death. My father was eighty-two when he came here from Lahore in '47, and when he died in '74, he was over a hundred and ten. The neighbourhood had a huge celebration for his funeral procession, and we even hired the Daulatram Band and gave away endless sweets.'

It was then he showed the palm of his hand to Chandrakant. 'The astrologer told me that I've got at least thirty-five more years. Then, after I turn one hundred and five, I'm gonna get me on that morning train, loud and high right up to the sky! But don't you worry, Chandu. Your job's even more secure than a government one.

'Wrap up the rest of this chicken for your wife and be on your way,' he said to Chandrakant in a hushed voice. 'I've got a working girl on her way, and she'll be here any second. You get to work over there in Jahangirpuri, and I'll get to work over here in Model Town.'

But the children of Chandrakant and Shobha never got as old as Gulshan Arora's. One after the other, the babies born to them in that half flat in bylane number seven kept dying. None lived longer than four months.

Not one or two, but seven babies in a row.

༄

It happened perhaps some winter's evening in 1995, some
ten years ago. I went to the Kwality Departmental Stores in
Vijaynagar. I had quit my day job five years prior and was then
as I am now a freelance Hindi writer.

I had my mortgage and other expenses to pay. Winter was
around the corner, and I still hadn't managed to buy warm
clothing for the kids. I myself had been wearing the very same
sweater twenty winters in a row. My wife hadn't been able to
treat herself to a nice sari or buy any jewellery since the day we
married. We avoided weddings since we lacked proper attire,
and couldn't afford a present for the bride and groom in any
case. We cut each piece of mango pickle into quarters, and
rinsed whatever slices of onion were left on the thali, saving
them for next time. We horded five rupee coins during the
year, saving them up to give away on Divali. I thought a few
times about ending it all, or running away, but then my kids
always brought me back. They were still in school. Books
came into my life like a curse, and took everything I had.
Sometimes it was the stories of Isaac Bashevis Singer, or else
Orwell's *Down and Out in Paris and London*, or Gorky's autobi-
ography – reading them brought me some respite. Maybe every
writer's fate is to live on the street, in the gutter. Or maybe I
just worried more than most because I wasn't famous and wasn't
important.

Whenever I sat down and opened a book or tried to write
something in those days, the full terror of my reality at home
cast a long shadow. I saw strange, sinister hues on the faces of my
wife and children that I couldn't pinpoint or understand. Death,

illness, penury, hearsay, and sorrow skulked through the house with heavy feet. At night sobbing sounds permeated the rooms and corridors. A cat screeched on the rooftop. The plaster was falling off the walls, and the doors opened and closed with a strange, sad groan.

It was also a time rife with illness: dengue fever, food poisoning, the flu. My wife had a thyroid problem, and our younger son was so thin, so frail, so shy and introverted, that we were racked with doubt about whether he would be able to take care of himself in the future. Ginsberg's 'Howl' and Muktibodh's 'In Darkness' echoed in my head. I woke up ten times a night. I considered the possibility that I had been duped and driven onto a surreal landscape of terror and nightmares, where each work of the honest writer puts his family in a condition more critical, makes them more unsafe – reality substituted by the awful surrealism of a poem.

The twentieth century was turning into the twenty-first, and with each new work I wrote, my life was plunged more deeply into the abyss. Delhi, along with the rest of the world, was changing fast, other capitals even faster. Here, only one beacon remained that still had any power, and it attracted cruelty, barbarity, greed, injustice, money – no other options were possible. When I tried explaining my troubles to Delhi's influential writers and thinkers, I felt as if I were a snail that had surfaced to the world above, telling the divine bipeds patting their fat bellies about his wild, weird, othercaste experiences from his home at the bottom of the sea. My language was incomprehensible. They viewed my utterances born of sorrow, vulnerability, and nerves with indifference, curiosity, wonder. They were of a totally different class. Their scraps were my meal. A poet had written something to that effect a few years ago, perhaps coping in similar circumstances.

In the middle of all this, I went one late afternoon to the general store in Vijaynagar where Chandrakant worked. The store was empty when I arrived, apart from Chandrakant, who I found lounging in the chair behind the counter singing an abhang devotional song. But there was a heartbreaking loneliness in his voice, as if he weren't singing for others, but as a crutch to steady himself. The previous July when I had gone to Pandharpur in Maharashtra on a film project I was shooting, I had seen the Gyaneshwar and Namdev pilgrim and chariot processions coming from Alandi. While sitting on the steps of the Vithoba temple I heard the abhang songs. The rain had just stopped a few moments earlier, but dark, menacing clouds still covered the sky. The voices of the singers in the shade, drenched from the monsoon humidity, were like a salve soothing my loneliness and vulnerability. Like a cure that fills vessels with a new blood of life. That day standing in the doorway at the store in Vijaynagar, I felt as if I was on the steps of the Vithoba temple rather than in Delhi.

Chandrakant didn't see me. His feet were stretched out on a stool in front of the chair, eyes closed, lost in the music.

'What a voice! Are you Marathi?' This was the first sentence I said to Chandrakant Thorat. He blushed.

'Are you looking for something?' This was the first sentence he said to me.

We introduced ourselves, and soon became friends. The two of us were trapped in our own respective hells. That first day I found out that he still hadn't become a father, despite having been married for so many years, and that one after the next his children had died from mysterious illnesses, as if cursed. None lived longer than four months. His wife Shobha was shattered.

The next week I went to his home: the half flat in bylane number seven, Jahangirpuri. Some of Shobha's hair had turned grey, and there was a hardness to her face, but she was still a beautiful woman. When she laughed, a softness sometimes peeked through. This, however, was rare. That night I listened to the whole story of their lives.

'You are the god Vitthoba, coming as you did just as I was singing the abhang…!' Chandrakant said, brimming with feeling. He assumed from my clothes and looks that I was a wealthy, connected, worldly man, capable of raising him out of the dark place where he was stuck. Chandrakant, Shobha, and the rest of the residents of bylane number seven for the most part came from one community. And I came from a different one. But my position in that community was no different from that of Chandrakant and others like him. There was no place for me in mine: I was nothing more than a mere writer. Many others came masquerading as writers, but I was the one shown the door.

We then met regularly. Chandrkant accompanied me to the Hasarat Nizamuddin Auliya shrine and sat on the marble floor where we quietly listened to the penniless qawwali singers sing their songs.

Mother! Let me go today!
Today is a day filled with colour
Festival of Colour, please let me go!

and

The path to the drinking well is very difficult
How can I fill my pot with nectar-water?

And I was amazed when one night after we'd had a little bit
to drink in their Jahangipuri half flat, Chandrakant reprised the
qawwalis. Shobha was busy cooking mutton dopyaza, and the
sweet smell of her cooking filling the flat. He was drumming
out the beat on empty plastic water bottles using two one-rupee
coins; his rhythm was flawless. He was as mesmerised with his
own music making as the qawwali singers had been with theirs.
I began tapping out the rhythm on the empty stainless steel
cup that I was drinking whisky from. Along with the exquisite
smell of the mutton dopyaza and, combined with the qawwali music, our meditation on Hazart Nizzamuddin, *mehboob-e
ilahi* – l'amoureux de la divinité – and the words of Amir
Khusrau, we felt the darkness dissipate. The whisky, too, had
lifted our spirits to the point that we were dipping and diving
in a pool of enchantment. Tears streamed from Chandrakant's
eyes. He didn't know that the writer of the qawwalis was the
master of the dargah where the two of us had gone several times,
and where Chandrakant, head covered by chador, prayed little
prayers that his life might improve. He prayed at the tomb of a
man he thought was a pir – a holy man – not a poet. It's true
that he was also a pir, the disciple of Auliya. We were there
one night when, once again, it was nighttime in the world all
around, and darkness blanketed us. The dawn of tomorrow
was drowned out in the dark like doused candles. We were
returning to our homes along the footpath with Amir Khusrau's
stick as our guide, groping in search of our life. Shobha, too,
was with us, perhaps trying to find her own, silently. I couldn't

stop wondering, who are these people present in the language of Khusrau – the man who first gave birth to poetry – and how did so many of them suddenly get there?

I wasn't able to see Chandrakant or Shobha for about a year after that night. Another book of mine came out during that time that chipped away further what tranquility I had left. Well-connected and high caste writers from Delhi, Bhopal, Lucknow and other major cities began calling me a rabid dog, fascist, copycat, thief, Naxalite, communalist, feudal, affluent. My newspaper column was dropped, payments cancelled, and the rumour mill spun out such awful stuff that I nearly went mad. They were dark days. My sleep was racked with nightmares. I felt as if my body, now skin-and-bones, was pushed up against the wall waiting for death in a solitary confinement cell in some labour camp, like Osip Mandelstam. Or sitting quietly on a chair in front of the Sharda mental hospital: a single grain of rice gets stuck in my windpipe, my breath grows erratic and I cast my eyes wildly around as my death approaches. Like the Hindi writer Shailesh Matiyani, who died in that hospital. Fascism was right in front of us with a new look. The power of illegal capital and criminal violence was hiding behind the veil of the great ideologies of the nineteenth and twentieth centuries, until it consumed and reduced to ash the great philosophies of the past two centuries in the irrepressible fire of its base ambitions and desires.

Sometime during that year I went for six months to Bombay and Pune in connection with a film I was writing. And even after I got back, I wasn't able to see Chandrakant for another seven or eight months: that's when I was busy editing a couple of small documentaries. The day-to-day struggles of getting by had, in some sense, led me to begin to forget about Chandrakant. And then one day I went to the Auliya shrine, thinking about going back to the village, a place where everyone escapes to run off to the big city, and where the fearful jaws of hunger, joblessness, and penury await every man who returns – when I sat down, alone, and saw that my friend Naim Nizami was sitting next to me with a smile.

'It's been forever since I've seen you here,' he said. 'Your friend who came with you, Chandrakant, he was here two months ago and arranged a twelve-thousand-rupee feast. And we were thinking of you. The biriyani was delicious.'

'Really?' I asked. Could Gulshan Arora, his seventy-year-old boss from the Kwality Departmental Stores have died and left him with two hundred thousand rupees? But Naim Nizami said that it was because his prayer had been fulfilled: he had become a father, even at his age. All on account of the mercy of Hazart Nizzamuddin, *mehboob-e ilahi* – l'amoureux de la divinité.

What else could I do that day but head straight for Jahangirpuri and Chandrakant's half flat? I arrived at dusk, sometime after five. Two planks of wood were bolted across the door, and a fat lock was fastened on the door chain. A board covered the 'balcony.' The woman who lived next door told me, 'They've gone to Saharanpur and will be back by Saturday. The baby's sick.'

I went again on Sunday, and this time found them. Worry lined Chandrakant's face, but what I thought had happened hadn't. Shobha was weeping. They told me that four months ago, Shobha had given birth to a baby boy in the nearby Kalpana Health Centre. The doctor was quite surprised that this middle aged woman, nearly an old woman, and who hadn't given birth in many years, could give birth to a baby whose vitals were perfectly normal. Shobha only needed a little stitching up. The baby was a fat eight-and-a-half pounds, and was rosy red. He was born on the fifth day of the tenth month. Chandrakant and Shobha's joy knew no bounds, and they returned home from the hospital. Shobha, having lost seven children before, was apprehensive. This time they wouldn't even let the most minor suspicion go unchecked, but the doctor told them every time they brought him in that the baby was healthier than health itself. There wasn't the slightest cause for alarm. Still, mother and child went in for the free checkup every week for two months. This time they wanted to take every precaution possible.

Some ten weeks passed like this. Chandrakant donated twelve thousand at Auliya's shrine for meals for the destitute. Shobha made a deal with Balaji of Tirupati: if the baby made it past twelve months without any problems, she would travel to Tirupati to perform the ceremonial head-shaving ceremony for the boy when he turned one, and would give the shorn hair to Balaji as an offering.

But one night Shobha heard the baby crying out as if in mysterious pain. Every breath he took was accompanied by a strange whistling-wheezing sound.

When she looked at the boy's face, she was amazed: she felt the baby was hiding his pain. He wasn't crying in the least, but silently fighting the pain on his own. Little furrows appeared on his forehead as if he were giving all he had in order to breathe each troubled breath.

It was two or three in the morning, and, now worried, Shobha woke up Chandrakant, who himself examined the infant. After another hour or two, the baby was again sleeping soundly, breathing deeply and regularly.

And the next morning, he was absolutely fine, drinking milk hungrily from Shobha's breasts until sated. Placing a finger beneath his lips caused him to burst into laughter, and he flashed his toothless gums. He began to recognise both mother and father, and Chandrakant's mind eased a bit. He said to Shobha, 'He probably had some mucus caught in his throat last night, and that's why he sounded like he had a whistle stuck in there. It's also been a lot colder lately, but I don't think it's something we need to worry about, it was probably just a mild cold. I'll mix a little bit of brandy in with his milk.' The hospital had given them a bottle full of brandy.

Shobha organised a small coal stove that would keep the baby warm from the damp chill outside. She hung a couple of old sheets and a rug from the top of the outside door frame to keep drafts out. Chandrakant sprinkled DDT powder and poured kerosene into the drainage ditch in front of their house in order to make sure mosquitoes and bacteria wouldn't breed. The two of them did everything that they could think of in order to be conscientious.

They named the boy Suryakant, and affectionately called him Suri.

This continued for a couple of weeks, until one night Shobha woke with a start to find Suri whimpering. Once again, his forehead bore the traces of intense pain, little wrinkles that ebbed and flowed as he silently struggled against deep discomfort, enduring the hurt, all alone. Any other child would have cried its eyes out.

She noticed that Suri kept trying to grab hold of his head.

Was his head in pain? She touched her palm to his forehead and it was like placing it over hot coals. He had a high fever and was burning up. Shobha shivered. *Not again! Not the eighth!*

She got up and turned on the light. The bulb was directly in front of the door and the light shone right into her eyes. Chandrakant woke up; he had been out late drinking with Gulshan Arora at his house.

Three months passed: Suri didn't utter a peep, let alone cry. His languishing face grew crimson, clay-coloured, expressionless, lost in pain. He wheezed like a whistle with each breath, and continually tried to grab hold of his head with his tiny hands.

In the light, Chandrakant and Shobha noticed that despite the severe chill, Suri kept kicking the blanket off his body, and drops of sweat glistened on his forehead.

Suri suddenly gave Chandrakant a look that gave him a start. The three-month-old boy who was quietly struggling with his suffering, looked at his father with a gaze that held both heartbreak and dignity – fathomless pain, but not begging for help. His own boy wore a face that told the story of a solitary struggle with hurt, a tiny, innocent face suggesting exhaustion at having lost a battle, or being stuck in a worry. *So this one too?* He nearly broke down.

'He's burning up,' Shobha said, taking Suri into her lap to try and soothe the boy. She froze. The boy's head dangled down as if his neck were lifeless, as if his head and torso were independent parts with no stable connection. Frightened, she placed her hand behind his head to steady it, unbuttoned her top, and placed his mouth flush to her breast. She was flustered and the only thing she could think of at the moment was to nurse him – it seemed like the most important thing in the world, and she hiccupped, on the verge of tears.

The baby's head on her chest felt like a pot out of the kiln. She nervously pressed her nipple into his mouth – it seemed he was hungry, or had at least found relief from his misery in her breast. Charged with great urgency, he alternately sucked on each breast in a nervous frenzy. Shobha was flush with a riot of maternal feeling for her boy, a sharp sensation that caused her nipples to swell and the blood in her body to rush in an urgent biochemical manufacture of milk to get it to the place where three-month-old Suri – in spite of his mysterious fever, inescapable pain and hunger – drank quietly and without crying. That night the sound of his gulping down his mother's milk could be heard echoing through the half flat. Shobha felt every vessel in her body had transformed into countless rivers of milk that served her swollen breasts. Her body quivered with a faint thrill. A primal, otherworldly, inscrutable music shot through the millions of cells and vessels in her body that transformed blood into baby's milk. Here in this world, only women can sense this music and understands its meaning.

A bit later Shobha was taken aback when she again put her hand on the forehead of Suryakant, still engrossed in nursing.

'Chandu… Chandu!' she called, her expression fixed between smile and surprise.

Suri's fever had gone down with astonishing speed – his forehead was growing cooler as if a painkiller had quickly taken effect.

Soon Suri's eyes were closed as he wandered peacefully through a dreamy sleep. Even in sleep his mouth again searched around for his mother's breasts.

And so he slept; it was four-thirty in the morning, with daybreak an hour or two away. Little licks of dawn fluttered in the air. Chandrakant had been watching the two for a long time without saying a word. Shobha came and lay next to Chandrakant, gently stroking Suri in her lap, who was deeply sleeping.

'I don't know why, but I feel a little scared,' she said, top still undone, weak voice filled with apprehension. She laid his hand across her chest, perhaps hoping for support from him.

'Let's take Suri to the doctor today no matter what kind of shape he's in,' Chandrakant said resolutely to comfort his wife. His hand found her breasts and touched them lovingly, excitedly, in deep gratitude. Sleep was now out of the question.

The first time he noticed her breasts was in Sarani, in the contractor's car, many years ago, when twenty-year-old Shobha, crying, had clutched his shirtsleeves, and in some frenzy had exposed her breasts to the nineteen-year-old Chandrakant, who had been looking at them with the bloodthirsty stare of a fanged, vicious beast.

And then that other day, that afternoon: they had only been in Delhi and in this neighbourhood for a little over a week when Shobha had been bathing on the balcony, under the tap, showering herself with the red plastic mug, covering herself not with water, but with a flowing screen of colour, and he saw her breasts. Chandrakant was drawn to her as if in the clutches of a magic magnet, simultaneously holding himself back while being drawn toward her.

And today! He still couldn't get over what he saw just a few moments ago: that otherworldly magic of hers. He still couldn't fathom what had happened. In the blink of an eye, these full, beautiful breasts had bestowed deep, carefree, blissful sleep on the three-month-old boy, now snatched away from the jaws of death, who had moments earlier writhed with high fever and endless torment, who had struggled with each breath. Goodness, what was in them? A healing potion? Nectar? Blessed offerings from Vithoba? A safe refuge for man or child, impoverished and alone, overpowered and helpless, worn down to the point of defeat in the struggle of life. He placed his lips there, reached up and began running his fingers through Shobha's tangled hair with warmth and affection.

And what happened then, again, was still a kind of magic. The blood in her countless veins and vessels that until a moment ago had transformed into milk and ran like a river into the mouth of little baby Suryakant now flowed like a hot, mad torrent. Mind and body were submerged into an irresistible music of primal excitement and irresistible titillation. The same blood was running like a river, this time where Chandrakant had placed his mouth.

'Chandu… Chandu,' she whispered as she pulled him on top of her with everything she had. Shobha's lust enveloped Chandrakant's mind, body, breath, eyes, skin. And her body, her scent, her weight, and the two of them. Chandrakant was breathing heavily but that was just the start of an otherworldly, magical, exceptional female game.

In that tiny half flat in Jahangirpuri bylane number seven, atop a magic carpet, the two of them rolled around, scorched by unseen flames of a fire that burned of itself in wordless play and that paradoxically also extinguished itself.

Suri lay an arm's length away, his little lips making little smiles that appeared and then disappeared, perhaps dreaming something in his carefree sleep.

Just over a half an hour later, when the millions-of-years-old sun began rising above the walls of the Galgotia English Public School in front of their house and the Shangra-La Hotel under construction behind it, and when the traffic began to grow thick on the National Highway, Chandrakant and Shobha, on top of the magic carpet, which wasn't really a carpet, just a cheap rug they had bought on the sidewalk bazaar at Vijaynagar, went limp and collapsed.

A HEAD THAT WON'T STOP GROWING

'Take this child to AIIMS,' said Dr. Anil Kumar Matta, the pediatric infectious disease specialist at Kalpana Health and Diagnostic Centre. 'They'll do a CT scan or an MRI. We could do it here, too, but since it's a private clinic, you'll have to pay out of your own pocket in a imaging facility in the market, and you don't have that kind of money.'

'Can you tell what the problem is, doctor?' Chandrakant asked, anxious.

'I don't know. His head is getting bigger and heavier. It's still in proportion to the rest of his body, but there's some abnormality, some imbalance. Don't wait, take him there as soon as you can, his life is in danger.'

Shobha and Chandrakant were distraught. Sometimes she snapped awake in the middle of the night to find Suri awake, too, in an odd silence, trying to press his palms against his heavy, hurting head. His innocent little face was crisscrossed with wrinkles of anguish. Every breath was a struggle, and she thought with each one, *this is it*: his delicate, immature lungs won't be able to draw in air next time. Meanwhile, Suri tried with all his might, his body twisting and turning. The baby's whistling, wheezing sound that had rent Chandrakant and Shobha's sleep, piercing them to their core, was Suri's will to live made manifest. *But what if he gets tired trying?* They couldn't bear the thought. *What are we supposed to do? Where are we going to get that kind of money?*

Shobha, anxious and feeling vulnerable, lifted Suri up, clasped his heavy head, and placed him in her lap. There was no doubt about it: his head was growing bigger and heavier every second of every day. She felt that a hot bag of lead and sand and iron were resting on her thighs, not a baby's head. She was getting sore, but there was nothing else for her to do but guide his mouth to her breast, and gently stroke his forehead. Chandrakant woke intermittently and helplessly watched the two of them, Shobha choking back her tears.

Chandrakant made enough money from working at Gulshan Arora's shop to scrape by each month. He was just able to pay for rent, bus fares, essentials, the electric bill. Shobha make a few rupees helping out with neighbours' wedding preparations, or making chutney, pickle, papadum. After Suri was born, their expenses went up, but she was no longer able to go out. I gave Chandrakant some money, and Gulshan Arora helped as well, adding that if he needed more he should just ask – after all, he had worked there for so long – and worry about paying it back later.

AIIMS – All India Institute of Medical Science – was a considerable distance from Jahangirpuri. And because it was government-run, treatment depended on who you knew and what connections you had. It was the ministers, high-ranking government officers, or the rich and powerful who had access to treatment at AIIMS. Chandrakant and Shobha stood hours waiting in the OPD with Suri in their lap. Either the number they had taken was never called, or perhaps it had been – but, amid the crowd, the doctor had seen Suryakant, looked at him indifferently, and told them to come back another day. After a huge runaround that lasted months, the doctor finally referred them for an MRI – only to discover that the 'machine wasn't working' at the hospital, and they would have to get it done privately. By then Chandrakant had understood: the doctors and staff were in cahoots and received a kickback for every patient sent to a private clinic. But it didn't matter. In the end, Shobha gathered all the jewellery from her mother, plus what she had taken from the contractor and inspector at Ramakant's, sold it all, and had the tests done.

By then, Suri was more than a year old, and his head had grown to a substantial size. It was true that his neck was stronger than before, and he could now use it to lift up his head. Either it would wobble for a bit before plopping back down, or he would slide on his knees and try to crawl. But pretty soon he tired and began fighting for breath. Whatever energy he had left over was spent trying to catch his breath, and he soon grew listless and collapsed in a heap wherever he happened to be.

But Chandrakant and Shobha had also recently begun to sense that it wasn't just his head that was growing, but that his mind, too, was developing more quickly than babies the same age.

Every day he seemed less and less like a baby.

Then I wasn't able to see Chandrakant for a few months. He did call once, and was at his wit's end. The doctors had more or less made their pronouncement. According to them, Suri would live at most one-and-a-half or two years. His disease was incurable. Of course, if they had two, two-and-a-half million rupees, something might be done. But to say that this was a sum beyond Shobha and Chandrakant's wildest dreams would be a gross understatement.

According to him, the doctors said that Suryakant was an abnormal baby and that the cells in his head were reproducing more quickly than the rest of his body, and that this was due to some unknown reason: a neurological disorder was possible, viral or bio-genetic factors could not be ruled out, a poisonous effect of strong environmental pollution could have played a part. Whatever the cause, if this disproportionate development wasn't stopped, in two-and-a-half-years max, Suri would surely meet his end.

But more than one year has already passed! Only six months left...?

I felt deep sympathy for Shobha and Chandrakant. They'd had a child together on the cusp of old age. But the child had a head like a time bomb sitting atop its own body. Tick, tick, tick, stuck in a countdown that would end its life with an explosion, always busy with plotting not its own life, but its death.

I couldn't bear looking at Suryakant. He began to recognise me, and when I arrived he smiled and tried to crawl over. I wondered how they did it, spending every second of the day with him. How they managed putting him to bed and waking him up, knowing that each new day brought his life one day closer to the end. What went through Shobha's mind when she breastfed him? Was the milk nourishing his life or was it fueling the flames of his impending death?

Shobha often wondered if the problem might lie with her, and she cast doubts on herself. Thirty years ago, she was gang-raped by the contractor, inspector, and Ramakant, her betrothed, as the men drank and drank, ate and ate, and watched porn. Her rectum had been shredded by the bottle inserted while on their savage spree. Maybe this had caused permanent strictures in her uterus? Could this be the cause of the seven deaths of her seven children? She couldn't talk openly with Chandrakant about these suspicions. It was only after her third child had died that she asked a nurse whether something in her womb might be spoiled?

The nurse looked Panjabi. She was plump, middle-aged, and clearly had an eye for making money. She gave Shobha a sharp look.

'I'm guessing you had an abortion before you got married? How many? You had your fun in bed. But now the bed's been made. You'll have to lie in it! Get an ultrasound done of your empty womb. Come see me tomorrow, I'll get it done for you. It'll cost seven fifty. Don't tell your husband. Otherwise forget it.'

But in those days Shobha had no way to scrape together seven hundred and fifty rupees.

A LIVING PUPPET OF STONE, STEEL, CLOTH, AND MUD
She breastfed little Suri. She tickled his chin and his under-arms – coochie coochie coo! She clapped her hands merrily and snapped her fingers, and made little bird whistles or cat sounds.

But Suri remained unmoved and showed almost no signs of life. She felt that death's shadow was gaining ground on the two of them, creeping up step by step. She saw in her mind's eye little Suri wheezing in her lap uncontrollably, then seizing up, going cold, his oversized head plopping down on her lap, lifeless.

She had a dream one night that while trying to lift Suri's head, it suddenly slipped from her hands, fell on the floor, and burst open. But instead of blood emptying from the head was every colour imaginable, flooding the floor and soaking the carpet – the one that was no ordinary rug, but the one they had called a magic carpet for thirty years, where she and Chandrakant had played their hot, primal games.

The still puzzling thing was that unlike other babies, Suri didn't cry at all. When he was hungry or needed something, he crawled over to Shobha. Whenever he fell down or got hurt, instead of bursting into tears he closed his eyes and pursed his lips as the pain disappeared inside. Then he touched the place on his body where he had been hurt, and then the thing he had bumped into. And once he got hurt and absorbed the shock, he wouldn't make the same mistake again. He learned from his experiences very quickly – so quickly that Shobha and Chandrakant couldn't believe it. It wasn't just the size of his head that kept getting bigger, but his brain was growing at a rate much faster than babies his age. It looked as if he was constantly thinking, absorbed in his silence, alone inside a secret darkness.

Suri not only didn't cry anymore, but he also stopped laughing. His expressionless face was like a marionette made of wood, cloth, stone, rusty iron. A weak, misshapen animated little puppet. It had to be a something out of the ordinary to make him laugh. Like one day when Shobha was looking for the knife to cut the veggies. Just a little while before she had taken the knife and placed it in the thali with the potatoes. But now the knife was no longer there; she searched high and low. Suri was in the corner, sitting up against the wall, silently observing her. Shobha, giving up finding the knife anywhere nearby, stood still. When she saw the knife along with a half-peeled potato hidden right where Suri was sitting, he was instantly filled with glee. At first she wasn't sure what to think, but then joined him in laughter.

One morning he crawled out onto the balcony and stared for a long time out at the houses around and the street below, all the while steadying his heavy head on his shoulders. It was exactly the time when all the kids were on their way to school, and the old folks were out buying bread and milk. Eighteen-month-old Suri seemed to be watching the hustle and bustle with great focus. A schoolboy of eight or nine came running carrying his knapsack, waiting on the side of the road for his school bus. He suddenly remembered something and ran off back where he had come from; the hustle and bustle of the street continued in the five or so minutes the boy was gone. Then the boy appeared again carrying a kids' water thermos. Suri thought this was hysterical. The boy looked up to see Suri laughing, and realised he was laughing at him because he knew he had forgotten his water bottle at home. The boy looked over to Shobha and shouted, 'Hey auntie! Your little boy is sooo cute. What's his name?'

'Suri!' she replied, smiling.

'Suri,' he repeated, waving and smiling as he walked toward the boy. But he stopped short when he saw the huge misshapen head. Shobha looked and saw Suri barely managing to wave with one hand, his face twitching, losing strength as he struggled. His lips formed the faint outline of a smile, but it was the strange expression of someone losing control.

Shobha was sure that Suri listened attentively whenever she and Chandrakant talked to each other. He stared at them, never blinking, as if he could understand each and every word.

That day, doctor Parvathi Nambiar of the Neurology Department at Jaipur Golden Hospital called Chandrakant and Shobha in private and told them with visible distress that Suri's continued survival had been a miracle of miracles, but that he could go at any moment, there was no telling. As far as she was concerned, his time was already up. Somehow, to them, this was the final word from a medical perspective about Suri.

The two were devastated. They avoided looking at one another, knowing that they wouldn't be able to endure the pain on the other's face. A kind of inner weeping inside them both kept them on edge. That night, the two of them sat at home in the half flat and spoke in such hushed whispers that it would have been nearly impossible for someone to listen in. Suddenly something in the corner of the room caught Shobha's eye. They had already turned off the light, and the room was dark except for a faint light from outside that cast diffuse light in the corner. She saw little Suri, sitting quietly leaning against the wall, watching them with stony, worried eyes that twinkled and flamed like little red marbles in the dark.

Shobha and Chandrakant believed that little Suri had both heard and understood everything they said.

His eyes peered at them from that dim corner of the room as if he had just been run over by a truck on the road, watching the living passersby as he lay dying: a last, lonely look. At that moment their son Suri's eyes had the cold, blank, hard stare of a corpse that had emerged from a sunken ship at the bottom of the ocean, and was suddenly standing on the beach, in the sun, gazing at the living.

Once I asked a doctor I knew if he had heard of this mysterious 'mangosil' disease. He said he'd never heard of it. Yes, there was a disease called 'meningocele,' but that had more to do with the spinal cord and lower back. It can cause hydrocephalus where the head can't drain the spinal fluid, and some swelling can occur. But there's a cure, and it's not fatal. The doctor continued, 'I can't find a disease with the symptoms you're describing in any of the medical literature. If a disease like that had been detected, it definitely would have been described in the literature – like when AIDS was first found in humans.'

Three years passed and more. Suri continued to live, putting paid to the predictions and prognostications of the doctors. Not only that, he grew more intelligent, focused, remarkable, and healthier than before. He even began to speak, with a lisp, and picked things up very quickly. He asked his mother about the letters he saw printed in books or on newspapers, and then tried copying them down with whatever paper was at hand. He tried to sketch whatever caught his eye: a bike, Shobha, a cat, dog, radio, fan, bus, cars, motorcycle, TV, tree, house – anything and everything.

Another development occurred during this time in the form of a twenty-one inch black and white Beltek TV that sat on

183

a wooden board fastened with nails to the front wall. It had a remote, which, for the most part, remained in the hands of none other than the misshapen three-and-a-half year old with the big head and little body. Chandrakant's boss, Gulshan Arora, had given him the TV set for free after he had bought himself a colour Onida in the meantime. Chandrakant got a cable hookup for the cheap price of sixty rupees, and then the TV had loads of channels.

Suri, three years and a few months old, sat for hours watching the TV, leaning against the wall, his massive, heavy head supported by his feeble shoulders, remote in hand. Shobha also liked watching some of the soap operas and channels that played Hindi film music. She finished her work and plopped down and was taken off guard in the beginning when Suri turned on the TV with the remote to exactly the channel she wanted to watch. The grey matter inside his malformed, dis-eased, ill-proportioned head was developed far beyond that of a typical three-year-old. He was able to read his mother's mind: all her wishes, all her thoughts. Like a spy he would look into the minds of those before him, and immediately know all their thoughts. Is this really the symptom of a disease, and one that the doctors say is incurable and puts Suri's life in danger?

Or is it something else entirely?

Chandrakant called me again one day. He told me that the night before he and Shobha had awoken with a start and found Suri wasn't in bed with them. He was in the corner against the wall watching TV at a very low volume – so low that it hadn't disturbed their sleep. It must have been after one in the morning. Chandrakant said what was unusual was that he wasn't watching cartoons or music videos, but had the news on. And that night, the reports of the nuclear tests at Pokhran were just coming in. He sat transfixed, his heavy, odd head sitting atop his little, weak body, as motionless as a statue of iron or stone. His twinkling red eyes were glued to the TV.

Chandrakant said that he felt fearful, and all sorts of notions about Suri popped up in his head. He was much older than his biological age. He was an oddity, this impossibly strange child. He knew things and kept thinking about things that we couldn't even guess. He couldn't be distracted like other kids with birds, toys, candy, kitty cats.

A few more months passed without my seeing Chandrakant or getting a call from him. I was getting tangled up with my own problems and stresses during that time. But then, out of the blue, he called at around three in the afternoon. His voice trembled with excitement.

Shobha had given birth to another baby boy. Normal, nothing out of the ordinary, healthy. Even though she was fifty Shobha didn't have any trouble in labor. The delivery was without incident. Chandrakant couldn't believe it when he was sitting outside in the waiting room and the nurse told him the news and asked for baksheesh. Maybe Auliya or Balaji had heard their prayers.

He then choked up a little bit. 'We decided a name right away. Amar – Amarkant. *The invincible.* Shobha is out of her mind with joy. Suri hasn't left his side for a second. You absolutely have to come and see the baby. Shobha's dying to see you. The day after Amar was born Gulshan Arora gave me fifty thousand to set aside for buying our own place, and I've talked to a bank about getting two hundred thousand as a loan. Maybe by next month we'll be able to move to the Janta Flats in Ashok Vihar.

I was stunned by this miracle of nature. By now Shobha was pushing fifty. Kids? At her age? Chandrakant kept talking over the phone. 'We won't be able to relax until you've come. Shobha insists and insists. Remember the first time we met and I was singing those abhang songs? Vithal had sent you, and everything changed once you came into our lives. Suryakant was also born after we met. I must have done terrible things in my last life that he's paying the price to free me from. Shobha says that if you don't come, Amarkant won't turn out right, either. So get here as soon as you can!'

Those were my toughest days, as tough as writers' lives often are. Days filled with panic, a feeling that everything was slipping away; nothing was stable, only stress after stress. I had no work at all, nothing saved for the future, no pension. Delhi was changing at an unbelievable pace. Every day new products would appear everywhere that no one could have ever dreamed of. The twentieth century had passed, and the new one was before us. And the dawns of the new one were unlike the dawns before. Only recently one of the greatest Hindi writers died in the Sharda mental hospital, mad and broke. A poet disappeared from home without a trace, and another had taken his own life. There was no place left for writers like me who wrote in this Hindi language. It was now an age of riches, power, violence, criminality, and looting, and it wasn't any less frightening than the worst nightmare you could imagine. Labour had no more value, and capital was no longer tied to labour – it was now totally free, untethered. My life was reduced to the struggle of how to get by. People like Chandrakant and me were more-or-less given a swift kick in the pants by society, who had no use for them under current circumstances.

No matter how bad things were, they could be worse. The shacks and makeshift houses of hundreds of thousands of people living in Delhi were very quietly, very secretively being set ablaze, their whole life reduced to ash. Or bulldozers were sent to destroy the houses, running them over until nothing was left but rubble. The people who lived there, poor and without work, were chased away. All 'revolutionary organisations' or cultural institutions were packed with developers, real estate agents, gentrifiers, high-ranking police officers, professors, intellectuals, commission men, all of whom banded together as one to starve to death anyone who dared describe what was going on.

I had been without a real job for fifteen years. I had degrees, important awards, job experience, good qualifications, but no matter what I applied for, I got turned down. The person they hired would be less educated, less experienced, but with good connections, ones in high places. A corrupt force had been spawned, and people like me could get nowhere near it.

I was down, very down, and sinking into despair.

I think another week must have gone until I was able to see them in Jahangirpuri. The road to get to house number E-3/1, bylane number seven, had changed. New buildings were under construction. Everything around was being torn down. Chandrakant told me that lots of people from the area were being evicted and sent to Bhilswa. They heard that a water theme park was going to be built in Jahangirpuri where all the rich kids in Delhi could enjoy their vacations swimming, splashing, snacking, horsing around, having a good time. He told me that he had put down one hundred thousand and taken out a loan for another two hundred for a third-floor public housing flat under construction in phase four of Ashok Vihar. It was a block of four-story apartment buildings for low-income residents. Chandrakant held the utmost gratitude towards his boss, Gulshan Arora, without whom this wouldn't have been possible. I thought to myself that Arora had probably also given him the money because it would be nearly impossible to find as honest and reliable a worker as Chandrakant. If he were forced to leave the half flat and move to another part of Delhi altogether, it would be impossible for him to continue working at Arora's shop.

My eyes lit on Suri. He had given me a big smile upon my arrival, sitting next to his newborn brother Amarkant, his heavy head wobbling up and down, planting little kisses on his brother and waving a torn rag in the air to chase off the flies. Shobha did not light the little coal stove: she made my tea on her new electric hot plate, my favourite kind of chai, steeped for a long time and very strong, with cardamom and ginger. And with so much sugar a diabetic wouldn't get near it with a ten foot pole.

EXPLODING COLOURS IN THE DARK AND THE MAGIC OF
THE CARPET

It was only because I came to visit that Chandrakant had taken the day off. It was getting close to five, and it wouldn't be long before night covered everything. The shadows of tall buildings slowly engulfed the little houses and bylanes of Jahangirpuri. The dark shadows from outside fell no less heavily on Chandrakant's family and me. I wanted to return home as soon as possible, but there was no way Chandrakant or Shobha were going to let me leave. It had been a long time – many years – since they spent days like these. It was the first time they were able to buy a place, their own home; at the ripe age of fifty, Shobha's giving birth to Amarkant, and, proving wrong the all-but-certain prognosis, was like the impossible made possible, as was the continuous, still-in-progress life of their firstborn, Suryakant.

Chandrakant took out a bottle of rum he had bought – Old Monk. He'd also bought a kilo of mutton he had chosen himself and had wrapped up from the Indian Halal Meat Shop: chops, thighs, rump, and legs, along with a container of fried-boiled spicy channa with green chilies, lemon juice, coriander, hari-patti, covered with thinly sliced onion.

'Tonight we're making mutton Kohalpuri for you. If it's too spicy you can wipe your face with a handkerchief,' Shobha chirped from beside her little stove, where the spices were browning in the pressure cooker. 'You'll never forget that once in your life you ate food cooked by Shobha!' She understood completely my darkness and despair. They wanted to share a little shining sliver of the good fortune and happiness they had found after so many years with me. And I was truly grateful.

'Hey Chandu, don't forget to pour a glass for me. As soon as I put the lid on this I'll come over and sit with you two,' Shobha said, then began to hum.

Giving birth to Amarkant, it was as if Shobha had sloughed off ten years off her body. Joy and hope had erased the lines on her face, the ones that years of struggle, deprivation, sorrow, poverty, and Suryakant's imminent death had carved in her face. Her eyes shone with the brilliance of a whole, free woman, and she radiated with every step. In the light of the forty watt bulb and glow from the stove, Shobha looked in that cramped little half flat like a young girl who had come directly from bathing in a cheery mountain waterfall. Her radiance and beauty right then gave off an energy that pulled my heartache and despair out of me, while pulling me toward her at an extremely high velocity.

I don't feel bashful and I'm not afraid to say that that night, I wanted to drown myself in Shobha's beauty and elation. Maybe some dormant animal lay inside me that had been lying ill in a corner, drowsy, tired and defeated, and was now suddenly aroused from sleep, glaring with hungry, greedy eyes at humming Shobha, who stood next to the cooker browning the spices. The fifty-year-old was transformed into a blissful girl.

Shobha turned with a start and caught my gaze, which drew her in. Her eyes locked on me for a moment before a twinkle of a smile again appeared. There was no anger, no reproach. Just the look of a woman who knew quite well how to coddle and tame the beast inside a man. The bold eyes of a relaxed, self-confident woman.

I noticed her looking at Chandrakant. They communicated wordlessly. He was spreading newspaper out over the carpet and setting down the plates and glasses. Suri was leaning up against the wall, heavy head propped up by his tired shoulders, channel surfing with the remote. One-month-old Amarkant was sleeping deeply in his little bedding.

Chandrakant slowly began to sing. *The colours today, the flowers today, O Ma the colours I see, my sweet one's home, the colours!* It was a colourful scene indeed inside that cramped little half flat that had for years mostly been under the dark shadow of want, disease, sorrow and anxiety. Technicolour bubbles, like the hues of Holi, coloured my mind and body, in and out, and ignited my desire. The three of us drank, the three of us sang. To the birth of Amarkant, to the life of Suryakant, to the joy

190

of moving to a new house, and to the radiance and festivity of the new mother Shobha. Chandrakant, embracing the fun of his drunkenness, put his arm around my shoulders and sang and sang.

Just then, Shobha looked at me – I hadn't moved my gaze from her – and then at Chandrakant. The two smiled from ear to ear, and then two things happened simultaneously: the steam valve on the pressure cooker gave out a long whistle, filling the room with a spicy aroma, and Shobha, taking a chiliful bite of the hot channa, leapt up. 'Ooh, ooh, hot! How many peppers did they put in this?' she said, puffing through the hot food in her mouth, before downing the glass of rum in one gulp. 'Chandu, how can we eat it like this? We need something to munch on if we want to finish the bottle, no?'

Chandrakant emptied his glass in a flash and stood up. 'I'll get some pakoras from around the corner, fish pakoras.' Looking at me, he said, 'You keep Shobha company and keep on drinking, I'll be right back.'

Then the TV channel changed and the volume got loud. It was a music video channel. I turned around to look and saw Suri propped up against the wall, remote in hand. He regarded me with a piercing gaze, and quietly stood as his x-ray-like stare penetrated my body, and I gave a little start. Suri took his father's finger, and, wobbling, accompanied him out the door of the half flat, his disproportionally large and heavy head resting like a time bomb atop his weak little body: every moment counting down – tick, tick, tick – to the moment (it could happen anytime) when it might explode, smashing this boy's life into smithereens. What hour and minute the timer is set for is anyone's guess.

Suri stopped on the balcony and turned that big head around to look at me. It was as if he was laughing with that strange twinkle in his eyes, an animated look of his very own, peering from beyond his impending death. Suri looked at Shobha again, gave a little wave with his right hand, then again took his father's hand before disappearing down the road and into the darkness.

Shobha was lost in her thoughts for a bit, then finished off her glass of rum in one big swig. It was her fourth glass. She wiped her mouth with her hands, took a bite of the spicy chili-lemon channa, and said between chews, 'Don't think of Suri as just a kid. He's a real imp. Nothing gets by him.' There was a devilish look in her eyes. I was a little rattled.

'Does he also know what goes through my head?' The buzz from the rum and magic carpet made my speech sparkle.

She came over beside me. 'Both Suri and Chandu know exactly what's on your mind and on my mind right at this very moment. Can you hide something like this? At this age?' She poured herself another little shot, and again downed it. 'What have we got in this life anyway? And if we do have something, someone else'll take it away. But whatever we might have left over, we can give to anyone we like. Don't you think so?' It came out slowly, deliberately. She leaned her head against my shoulder. 'Look how old I am, look how old Chandu is, and we just had a baby, we've just bought a house. A fifteen-year mortgage. Do you think we'll even be around to see it paid off? I look behind me and I'm tired. I look behind and I'm scared.

I'm exhausted. And Suri – how long can he keep gasping for breath? He was in bad shape again the other night. His head hurts like hell, but he never says anything, he just keeps fighting, all night, him versus death. Sometimes I think that the almighty should either just cure him once and for all, or he should…'

She began to shake. I consolingly stroked her hair as her tears streamed down onto my shoulders.

'And now Amarkant! See the kinds of games he plays. You know how old I was when I gave birth to him? But how long will Chandu and I be able to live with him? It's frightening. How will he manage after we're gone? How will he pay off the rest of the mortgage?

We were sitting on the carpet that used to ignite the flames that Shobha and Chandu put out with their games spanning many years. That day, too, the flames grew more aroused, the light of the fire giving off sorrowful hues for a few moments in the darkness of that half flat. Then the flames caught and bloomed into resplendent colour; two of us were shocked and delighted. And then our fever grew even hotter, until the pressure cooker blew its whistle for the fourth or fifth time.

Chandrakant came back with fish pakoras, peanut snack mix, and a handful of other goodies. Suri was slurping on an icypole. He ambled over to me, hopped in my lap, and rested his heavy head on my shoulder; the same spot his mother had wet with her tears a few moments ago. The weight of his head sent a shiver through my body. The great pain he must suffer, and the endless torment!

I gently tickled his forehead for a little while, then gave him a kiss. Straining, he lifted his neck, smiled at me for a moment, then hopped off, grabbed the remote, and sat again in the corner, back propped against the wall.

Chandrakant filled our glasses and spread out the pakoras, peanuts, and onions in front of us on newspaper. Shobha joined us after turning off the stove.

It was the kind of night when the three of us understood that our lives were interwoven as one by fate and other forces beyond our control. The same road led to our liberation and our mortality.

Chandrakant alternately sang abhang songs and Khusrau songs.

I noticed Suri had changed the channel. He put on the BBC, and Bill Clinton was on. I think this was an evening in 1998 – could it have been during the impeachment proceedings?

The 'Mangosil' virus and an ant

That night of December, 1998, had receded into the past. Days were racing by, and the world outside was changing at the same fast pace. The streets of Delhi were getting widened. Little bylanes and narrow backways were vanishing. Who could keep track of all the flyovers being built? Hundreds of thousands of cars of all shapes, sizes, and models flooded the streets. Everywhere you went it was the same: four wheel drives, honking horns, exhaust fumes. And *speed*. It was impossible to walk anywhere, and cyclists and scooterists were getting run over every day. These fatal accidents didn't even make the TV news, or get in the paper. Hundreds of villages like Jahangirpuri, Mangolpur, Loni, Nazafgarh, Harinagar, Ziyasrai, Bersarai, Karkarduma, Prahaladgarhi simply ceased to exist and were erased from the map. And where they once were? Malls, multiplex cinemas, hotels, markets, more stores, parks, banks, gated communities, gas stations. You couldn't go a month without a neighbourhood changing so utterly that you wondered if you were remembering it right.

The residents of the makeshift house built in Jahangirpuri's bylane number seven had disappeared, and no one knew where. Thousands of poor, lower-class families living in the neighbourhood had been displaced. The police, local authorities, powers-that-be – all were gung-ho to build buildings and make markets with their bulldozers, teargas, and politics. Modest houses and the less well-off were wiped out of neighbourhoods all over the capital city. Violence, crime, and power – sinister, inhuman – spread everywhere. The population of Delhi had crossed the twelve million mark. Of those, some ten million had neither a secure livelihood nor any savings for the future. The homes they lived in weren't their own. A bank, either private or foreign, held the mortgage and deed. Countless people worked like indentured labourers just to be able to pay off loans or mortgages.

Chandrakant, Shobha and family moved to the public housing flat they bought at C-7/3, Ambedkar Nagar Colony, Phase Four, Ashok Vihar. I was enlisted to help move them from Jahangirpuri. They had amassed so much stuff over the years that it took four trips in a Tata 407 to move it all.

195

In the meantime, I had been diagnosed with bone tuber-culosis, and several of my vertebrae had fused. I was confined to bed for ten months, and the treatment cost a small fortune. We had to sell the old house and move to a new one. During this time, I also wrote a book in a kind of frenzy, one that took each and every last moment of free time. The language I wrote in and read, spoke and thought had turned into a kind of torturous cage. I felt the fascist nails and menacing claws of in-your-face corruption, violent casteism, and stalking injustice everywhere in my life. I was turned down for every job I applied for. My degrees, experience, and body of work no longer had any meaning. All of the great ideas and ideals of the nineteenth and twentieth centuries had become tools to play with in the hands of power brokers, base hypocrites, arse kissers, high-class schemers. Those who killed, killed in the open. Thugs committed their thuggery in the public eye, with a spring in their step. Bribes and kickbacks were counted out continuously, in front of the camera or behind. Cultural institutions had been taken over by gangs of plunderers, who let themselves be feted on the dais, gave speeches, and laughed all the way to the bank. A dark, frightening cloud of reality had descended, one that no one had expected.

Reports of what was really happening were so obscene, so rotten, that bringing them into a poem or short story would simply ruin the poem or the short story. So most poets and writers avoided writing about what went on – but they kept on writing, and kept on winning awards.

So, please come with me, and we'll desist for now with these accounts of what's going on, and instead travel to Ambedkar

Nagar public housing flat C-7/3, Ashok Vihar, where Shobha and her family now reside.

Amarkant was five by now, and had started attending Blue Bells school. Shobha had purchased a sewing machine. She sewed for friends and neighbours, and took home fabric from a few shops in the bazaar to stitch – the mortgage payment and school fees were due at the beginning of each month. Gulshan Arora died in the meantime, and his son Kishan had sold the shop in Vijaynagar. Chandrakant found work in another shop in Deep Market in Ashok Vihar. Every day he walked to and from work.

I had moved right outside Delhi with my family, to Ghaziabad. Chandrakant had my new address and number.

I had a premonition that at any moment Chandrakant might call me with news of Suri's death. He was by now eight years old. Not only was he still alive, having improbably fought and confounded his date with death, but the mind inside his malformed, ill-proportioned, misshapen head was so remarkable and strangely curious that anyone who heard him talk was stunned, confounded, flabbergasted.

For example, one day he said to Shobha, 'Ma, you're spending your eyesight so you can make Amar's school fees. If you would only sell your eyes, you could put him in a cheaper school.'

One night Shobha awoke to find Suri on the balcony wrapping twine around his head. His lips were shut tight, and his face was wrinkled up in pain. His lungs were making that whistling sound while he tried with all his might to breathe in the outside air. His eyes were red and bulging. When Shobha came to him and placed her hand on his back he said in his hoarse voice, 'Doctors only know how to cure diseases that would cure themselves anyway, without any treatment.' He struggled to take a breath, and then let out a deep sigh. 'Hospitals are built for the same people that cars, hotels, airplanes, and big buildings are built for.'

One day he announced, 'The disease inside of me is because of that dirty drainage ditch in front of our half flat.' He looked off into the distance for a bit before adding gravely, '"Mangosil" is the name of the disease, and the virus that causes it is called, do you know? Poverty.'

One day when Amar was going to school, Suri said, 'No matter how much kids study in school, they could learn more without school. People who send their kids to school are those who want to get rid of them.' Again a vacant look came over his face for a bit and then he added, in the manner of a philosopher, 'What is true is that those who are more well-educated inevitably work as underlings or servants for those less well-educated. School is a servant factory. The most powerful, richest, and best-off people in the world are always less well-educated.'

Suri, because of his illness, studied at home. He read the paper, watched TV, listened to the radio, and began going to the Jupiter Network cyber café in nearby Neemri market. Everyone in the area began to recognise him: the shape of his body, with the skinny trunk, oversized head, and funny way of walking.

One day Suri said, 'The reason that people stare at me is that they've never seen an ant, with its big head, dressed in man's clothing.' He said this without laughing, but with eyes red, lips parched, and trembling a little. He continued, 'Only ten to twenty per cent of people in this world are human. The rest are ants, cockroaches, dogs, pigs, or oxen.' He flashed an ironic smile. 'I mean, look at this family. Papa's an ox, Mummy is a machine, and Amar's a cockroach. And I'm just a little worm that crawled out of the gutter one night and snuck into Mummy's belly.'

In the middle of the night one night, Suri's hands were pressing against the sides of his head, struggling to take each breath. 'My head keeps getting bigger because it keeps knowing things little heads can't know, or don't want to. If they tried knowing them, their heads would grow as big as mine.'

Red flashed from his eyes like sparks. 'I know full well that the US invaded Iraq only for the oil. But they'll be able to buy in oil whatever they've spent to hide this fact. The US would invade India, too, if they extracted that much oil. Just wait, one day either the whole world will equal the US, or it'll be the whole world minus the US.'

One night Suri, who was almost eight-and-a-half, was writhing in pain, crying like any other kid his age. It was the first time he acted like this. Normally when in pain he went out quietly and fought the pain on his own. He lay down and put his head in his mother's lap. 'Mummy, just find me some poison,' he whimpered. 'I can't take it anymore.' His tears wouldn't stop. In between sobs he said, 'I just don't understand why people are born whose lives are filled with so much hurt.' A little while later his pain subsided. 'Mummy, I need a pill the size of the sun to make the pain go away.' Then, still in tears, 'Tell Papa I want to live, Mummy. I don't want to die yet. Not this soon. There's no way we might be able to find the money to be able to afford to cure me?'

Suri's voice was full of such hopelessness and longing. Shobha caressed her son's head in her lap and herself started to weep. What could she possibly do to save the life of her son? Ideas failed her.

That night Shobha had a deep change of heart. She calculated that even if they sold the house and everything they owned, and recovered their mortgage, they would still be short of the one-and-a-half or two million they needed to have Suri treated properly, or even cured. Their only recourse was to offer their prayers, which they did anyway. And it was only due to the grace of god that Suri was still alive. She decided that from that day forward, she would try to focus less attention on Suri's eventual death and create space for him where he didn't have to be continuously traumatised by his 'fixed mortality.' She told Chandrakant her idea.

Suri started watching movies on the VCR like *Qayamat se Qayamat Tak*, *Lagaan*, *Devdas*, *Main Hoon Na*, *Kaun*. Shobha and Chandrakant took him to out to the movies a couple of times. Both of them were acutely aware that Suri was only going to live as long as he was going to live. So they wanted him to give him as many experiences as they could, within their means. Sweets, chaat, pizza, hamburgers, Pepsi, Coca Cola, amusement parks like Appu Ghar, the zoo, the Qutub Minar.

Chandrakant told me about a truck that had run off the road and hit a tree. The driver was killed, and his passenger was taken to the hospital. Chandrakant, Shobha and Suri were on their way home in a rickshaw. Suri too saw the tree and almost ran to it; its trunk was damaged in several places. Suri kept quiet for a while before saying, 'The tree is always silent, sitting in its own spot. Even if it wanted to fight someone, like that tree, it would only be to save itself.'

Even though Suri's strange, tangled thoughts deeply vexed people, Chandrakant and Shohba felt sometimes the real kid inside would emerge, the one that was simply and straight-forwardly a child his own age, with the same wishes, desires, obstinacy, tantrums. He was often quite stubborn about getting to eat the foods he liked. Like besin sweets, red amaranth, fried moong.

Sometimes when people paid more attention to Amar, they saw the envy and jealousy in Suri's eyes. It was true that five-year-old Amar had more stuff than his older brother, Suri. The main reason was that he went to school. He had a cute little vinyl backpack with Donald Duck and Roger Rabbit on it. Plus notebooks and lots of books with all sorts of pretty pictures. Amar also had more clothes. He had two changes of his school uniform, two pairs of socks, one pair of shoes, two ties. He had a nice little blue square tiffin lunchbox that held another little compartment inside. Shobha packed parathas in the tiffin and put a few cookies in the compartment inside. He also had a red water bottle in the shape of an elephant and if you lifted up its trunk it sprayed blue water.

Seven was the time Amar normally left home for school, and Shobha and Chandrakant spent an hour getting him ready. They were totally focused on Amar, who had begun to try getting out of going to school. While getting him ready they had no time to pay attention to Suri.

The Blue Bells school bus stopped right out front; the bus was packed with other schoolboys and girls. Sometimes Shobha, but mostly Chandrakant, would go out to put Amar on the bus. After he got on and said 'ta ta' and the bus pulled away they went back inside.

Every once in awhile Suri too tagged along to see Amar off, ambling far behind the others with his hunched shoulders bearing the load of his heavy, misshapen head. The boys and girls lit on Amar as he approached, giggling and calling out to him, waving and telling him to hurry up. Suri watched this silently, breaking into a happy smile. But then he felt that some of the kids and the girls in particular were looking at his weird head – the kids got a little scared, they began pointing at him and whispering things to each other, and this frightened Suri. After that, he didn't come back for a few days and just stayed home. Then, after a little while, he would try again.

In the morning Shobha sometimes noticed Suri looking covetously at his brother when he was getting dressed for school, putting on his crisp, white, freshly washed shirt, blue shorts and red tie, with matching white socks and shiny black shoes. She was assailed by ugly thoughts. After all, Suri was not well. There was no question that he was not healthy or normal. What would happen if he did something to himself because he felt frustrated, or deprived? Or what if he got angry and jealous of his brother and went and did something stupid. It was true, though, that compared to Amar, Suri didn't have much stuff. A couple of t-shirts, two pairs of shorts, a pair of sweatpants. And all cheap stuff at that. His shoes, too, were nothing special, just some dull grey no-name sneakers she had bought on the street. Every morning, Shobha nagged and nagged Amar to brush his teeth, and even had to squeeze the Colgate herself onto the toothbrush. Then there was Suri, who did everything on his own. He liked the cool minty taste and smell so much that one time he squeezed a little extra onto his brush; Shobha saw, and yelled at him. 'Hey, do you think that's candy? Easy does it!'

Suri froze. He never did it again. Then there was the time Amar had got ready for school and set off with Chandrakant, leaving Suri alone with her, and he said, 'Mummy, you're right to think the way that you do. Why waste good money for no reason buying clothes and shoes for someone whose life you don't put any stock in? I think you should do something similar with that someone's food. Who knows when he might die? Until then who knows if he's properly digesting the food he eats?'

Shobha couldn't believe what she heard. 'Have you lost your mind again? Always thinking crazy thoughts?' She ran her hand along Suri's head. His eyes welled with tears. 'Son, as far as life and death go, nobody knows when and where you go forwards or backwards. The doctors only gave you until two or two-and-a-half, but you're still with us, thanks to the grace of Auliya and Vitthal. And look at your papa's boss, Gulshan Arora, who said that after he turn one hundred and five, he would ride that morning train, loud and high into the sky. He didn't even make it to eighty. He folded long before.'

Suri found this hysterical. 'Mummy, if I live to be one hundred and five, can you imagine how big my head would be? And where would I live? And who would come to lift that head of mine?'

~

Amar didn't go to school on Sundays. Suri stomped his feet like a little kid: he wanted to take Amar's tiffin, packed with parathas, go to the park, and sit on a bench under the neem tree and eat them. For his outing, Shobha packed two parathas, potato curry, and two cookies. Suri also brought a water bottle along. The crisis began when Amar noticed his brother making off with his tiffin and his water bottle; weeping and wailing ensued. The brothers began pushing and shoving each other. Suri would have strangled Amar if Shobha hadn't come swiftly to remove his hands from his throat. That day, Shobha saw a wildness in Suri's eyes, as in a writhing, wounded animal that suddenly exhibits savagery.

Suri looked right at Shobha and said in a cold, unwavering voice, 'I want a tiffin box of my own. And you, all you living people, will buy one for me. From now on, I won't be eating lunch inside this house.'

From then on Suri took his lunch box and tottered down the steps.

The truth was, however, that these kinds of incidents were few and far between. Most of the time Suryakant was nothing but loving and affectionate with his younger brother, Amarkant. And after he started going to the Jupiter Network cyber café, he began bringing back toffees, magic pop ups, and chocolate bars for his brother; it turned out that the owner, Rohan Chawla, gave him money. Chandrakant told me that Rohan told him his son Suri had a 'genius mind.' He added that if he didn't have any work to do at home, he could go spend time at the café, and he'd be happy to pay him seven or eight hundred a month. Suri was a quick learner on the computer, and picked up Photoshop, learned how to blog, and do some graphic design work. He started learning 3-D animation on his own, without help from others; Rahul Chawla was awestruck.

Suri helped Amar when he had homework. When he had drawing assignments, Suri would draw them or colour them in with crayons or coloured pencils so vividly that Amar inevitably got 'very good' or 'excellent' marks. But one time Shobha yelled at him, 'If you do all of your brother's work, what's he gonna learn? Let him do his own work!' Suri stopped what he was doing and stood up.

'Mummy, I want you to know that the drawing of the little shack and tree and sunset I've just made is the last picture I'll ever draw.' He staggered over the balcony and quietly went outside.

Shobha took a deep breath.

There are two other important facts about Suryakant. One is that he began sleeping less and less. It may have been that he did what ever he could to put off going to sleep – reading, watching TV – since the headaches and breathing problems were at their worst after he got up. One good thing about the new place was that the TV was in the living room.

The other key fact was that Suri was studying English and learning fast. He began watching English-language channels and reading books and newspapers in English. Sometimes he called me and we had long talks; Rohan Chawla let him use the phone at Jupiter Networks as much as he wanted. Suri surfed the internet and did a lot of instant messaging.

He called me one day. 'Uncle, I've got the idea that before Independence, it made more sense to study Hindi. Now it's better to be able to speak English.' He paused to think about what he just said. 'When the English were here, it was English that made us into slaves. Now that the English are gone, it's Hindi that's turned us into slaves.'

This is how he talked. Another time he told me, 'Uncle, there's no such thing as the Third World. There are only two worlds, and both of them exist everywhere. In one live those who create injustice, and all the rest, the ones who have to put up with the injustice, live in the other.

Much later I found out that Suryakant had kept a diary. He wrote all sorts of stuff in both Hindi and English. It looks like he wrote down his thoughts in the notebook, or what he was reading. The notebook was pretty thick, and mostly filled up with, it can be surmised, what he read and thought.

He had lovely handwriting, in both English and Hindi. From page twenty-seven of his notebook:

(in English)
Everything is looted, spoiled, despoiled,
Death flickering his black wing,
Anguish, hunger – then why this lightness
overlaying everything...

(in Hindi)
I am trying to remember who these lines belong to. Are they
Anna Akhmatova's?

From page thirty-two:
*They've erased all my words from everywhere, and now I have
died, absolutely died, my huge huge head, with its pain inside
that can't be cured, bullet marks and blood stains all around,
and everywhere people are eating, people are laughing, didn't
they get the gruesome news, or are they part of the crime?
They're counting the money on camera and off and I am
wondering whether my head is India that's slowly dying...?*

Shobha and Chandrakant didn't really understand the writings
of their sick child, Suryakant. The two of them couldn't read
and write very well, and didn't know English at all. They only
spoke Hindi and Marathi, and lived a very meek existence.
Chandrakant once said to me, 'You've definitely left your mark
on Suri. He's always reading your books, and he's always marking up the pages.'

Shobha told me in tears that just about a week ago he said
that there was something he had read in one of uncle's books he
wanted to come over and ask about.

But I'll never find out what it was in which book of mine
he wanted to find out about. He died before he could ask.

It was the death that for the past six years everyone had
feared might happen at any moment. Suryakant had fought
mightily on his own behalf to stay alive and stave death off.

Every night Suri held back the clock hands of the time
bomb in his head, buying himself a day or two more. He was
unwavering in his efforts. It was a desire to live shared by tens
of millions of others who suffer injustice and live inordinately
difficult lives.

But one day Suri decided he was done and gave up.

How? Why? This is what Chandrakant and Shobha told me as we were coming back from Nigambodh Ghat, where Suri's last rites were performed.

A HAWKER, SUN ON THE ROOFTOP, THE PRESSURE COOKER'S WHISTLE THAT WHISTLES AND WHISTLES, AND A CHINESE CAP GUN The date was 25 December, 2004.

The high temperature in Delhi on that day was sixteen degrees centigrade, and the low was three point four.

Even at nine thirty in the morning, fog was so thick that that there still was no trace of the sun. Cars on the road at eight still had their headlights on, and were crawling along like ants. Visibility was almost zero; you couldn't see more than a few metres ahead.

Chandrakant, after waiting forty-five minutes outside with Amar for the Blue Bells bus that never came, returned home.

Suddenly around ten the fog lifted, and the bright, shining sun revealed itself. Shobha was making channa dhal in the pressure cooker that day. As soon as the sun came out, all the women who lived in the C-block apartment building scurried up to the rooftop. Shobha took her sewing machine and carpet and went to the roof, too – not the same carpet as the magic carpet from Jahangirpuri, but one she bought after they had moved to Ashok Vihar. She was up sewing until two-thirty the night before. She had been wearing glasses for the past five years. She had until three that day to finish sewing fabric for a store called Kalpana Boutique and Design Garments in Deep Market. With the deadline, she was stressed out and in a rush.

She spread out the rug and sat with her sewing machine. She was half listening for the sound of the steam whistle on the pressure cooker with the channa dhal she had put on. It could blow at any moment. She would count how many times the whistle blew, and run down and turn off the stove when it went off for the eighth time.

Suri and Amar were sitting with her on the rug. Suri was writing something in Amar's notebook, and Amar was leaning over, watching quietly. That's when Bimla Sahu, who was sitting just a little distance away, said, 'Your oldest one has been spitting off the balcony and ripping up paper into little bits and throwing them off like confetti. Tell him to stop. I've also found peanut shells and candy wrappers outside my door a few times.'

Bimla Sahu had announced this deliberately loud enough so that all the other women sitting on the rooftop would hear.

Suri, who had been hunched over Amar's notebook writing something, also listened. He lifted his giant head and said hoarsely, 'That's not true, Auntie! I've never thrown anything off the balcony. And I've definitely never spat off it. Do you really think I'm that uncouth and stupid?'

That was enough to make Bimla Sahu, who had such a sturdy frame the women of the Janta Flats called her 'the wrestler' or 'toughie,' turned several shades darker. Then she let loose.

'Oh, look who's using his big mouth! Everything I said you do – you know you do! You yellow cowardly little kid!'

Suri's breathing quickened. 'You're lying, Auntie. And you don't know how to do anything except make drama. When's the last time you had your blood pressure checked?'

No sooner had he said this than Bimla Sahu clanged down the thali from which she was picking out pebbles from the rice.

She screamed and gestured with her hands, 'Oh, are you gonna check my blood pressure? Why don't you fix that jug of a head of yours first? You probably don't even realize you're drooling off the balcony. If you have to go out on the balcony, stand on the right side. D'you have to stand right over my head?'

Pain was written all over Suri's face. His lips began to tremble and he was having difficulty breathing; all of this frightened Shobha. She hoped this wasn't the start of one of Suri's massive headaches. He was an extremely sensitive boy, and Bimla Sahu had really got to him.

Shobha made sure the other women could hear as she shot back. 'Hey little miss tough stuff, why do you have to pick fights with little kids? If you need someone to fight with, don't forget *you can count on me!*'

The emphasis she put on *you can count on me*, the title of a popular film those days, was so good that the women on the roof top broke into hysterics. The tide of laughter was so powerful that it swept up Amar and Suri, too.

And, finally, tough–stuff–wrestler Bimla Sahu herself wasn't immune to its force. 'Not bad. If Shah Rukh sees your moves he'll cart you off to elope.' She then returned to picking pebbles out of her rice.

Just then – it must have been five or six minutes after eleven – the shout of the street hawker came from below. The C-block apartment building was five stories tall. All of the apartments' roofs were connected; Amar, along with the other kids, ran over to the railing.

Suri also lumbered over to the edge, with his heavy, mis-shapen head.

Pickle-pee! Pickle-pee! Pickle-pee! The street hawker played his little plastic flute below. A lengthy bamboo stick was tied vertically to the handlebars of his bike; fastened to the stick was a cardboard sheet at least four-feet-by-four-feet. All sorts of fabulous items hung from it: balloons, toys, assorted colours of plastic combs, lighters, scissors, berets, drawstrings for skirts, ribbons of rainbow colours, hair bands, hair brushes, little mirrors, bangles, and all sorts of other merchandise.

But at the very top of the board sat a row of Chinese cap guns. You could get them in any bazaar those days for fifteen rupees, and they were unbelievably popular with the kids of Delhi. Chinese goods were threatening to flood the marketplace – wondrous electronics at startlingly low prices. The Chinese cap gun shot little plastic coloured bullets, and as soon as you pulled the trigger, rat-a-tat, ping! ping! Utterly realistic. And if you aimed right, the plastic bullet would hit the target spot on.

'I want a Chinese cap gun so I can kill the bad guy!' Amar pleaded.

Shobha had earlier said no. But, number one, just yesterday, she received 2,200 rupees from the Kalpana Boutique Garments Centre, part in advance, the rest on receipt. And, number two, Bimla Sahu and her yelling and screaming had put her and the kids in a really foul mood, and she thought the kids might feel better if they got to play around. Therefore, she decided to purchase a cap gun. She went up to the railing, leaned over, and shouted to the hawker. 'Hey mister! Don't move, I'm coming right down.'

Shobha was just about to go down the stairs when she heard Suri's cold, hard, machine-like voice.

'Mummy, I want a cap gun, too. My own.'

Shobha turned around to find Suri pressed against the railing, standing and looking at her with the big head held up by his shoulders.

'Are you just a little kid who likes to play guns?' she said with a sweet smile.

She reached their flat (C-7/3) on the third floor, unlocked it, went in, took money from the pouch inside the cabinet drawer, and took the stairs down to the ground floor.

When she got there, she bought the Chinese pistol from the hawker for fifteen rupees. She tried and tried to bargain, but he wouldn't even drop the price one rupee. Shobha thought, they're not going to drop the price of these things that are selling like hotcakes. She took the gun, went up the stairs, and, when she got to their flat, found Amar who had come down from the roof. You could see on his face how happy and excited he was. He grabbed the cap gun at once and rushed back upstairs. Shobha shouted after him.

'Be sure to let your brother play with it, too! Don't play on your own.'

'It's mine, mine!' Amar shot back while running.

Shobha went into the kitchen. The pressure cooker with the channa dhal sat atop the gas burner. They purchased a gas burner after moving to Ambedkar Nagar from Jahangirpuri, retiring the old coal stove, though there were still plenty of families in the Janta Flats who still cooked with coal or kerosene.

Today for lunch she was planning to serve the channa dhal and ghiya dish that she, Suri, Amar, and Chandu all really liked. She learned the recipe in Jahangirpuri from Natho Chaudhuri, who had left her alcoholic husband in Bijnor and run away with her lover to Delhi. She called the dish 'luckdala.' Maybe she got 'luck' from the vegetable 'loki' and 'dala' from 'dhal,' and combined the two to come up with this cute name. She thought she would wait until the pressure cooker had let off all its steam so she could go back to her sewing on the roof without worrying. There were still ten or so minutes before noon. She turned the gas up on the burner.

One minute later the cooker gave off its first steam whistle – a long, throaty blast. There was probably still plenty of steam bottled up inside. The strong burst of vapor carried spicy, delicious smells throughout the kitchen, smells that made Shobha's mouth water. But still five more whistles to go.

Just as the second whistle was about to blow, she heard a loud commotion outside. Women and children, screaming and shrieking, the sounds of people running downstairs.

Shobha froze. Something terrible had happened. She first thought of Amar and was seized by fear.

She turned off the burner and started fast for the roof. She thought about what Suri said just after she called after the hawker, *Mummy, I want a cap gun, too. My own*, in that cold, hard, machine-like voice, eyes red, head trembling, that look of wildness on his face, just like when he took Amar's tiffin box to eat in the park, and got in a fight with Amar, and if she hadn't broken it up Suri would have strangled his little brother.

And now if Suri had pushed Amar off the roof?

'Amar! Amar!' she shouted, arriving on the roof in bad shape.

Amar clung to the railing as if he were made of stone, sobbing quietly, holding the Chinese cap gun in one hand.

The women still on the roof leaned over the railing and stared down.

Shobha looked. There was a crowd of people gathered around the spot where just moments earlier the hawker had stood with his bike. More people came running from adjacent apartment buildings.

Bimla Sahu, the one who everyone called 'toughie' or 'the wrestler' since she was big and strong and always picking fights came up behind Shobha, put her hand on her shoulder, and she was in tears.

'He went up to the railing himself and just jumped. It happened so quickly.'

Her face was covered in tears and she was choking on her sobs. 'Your eldest committed suicide! You and I said one little thing, and look how he took it to heart.'

The women said Amar came back to the roof with his cap gun, and as soon as he fired the first shot, Suri began to have trouble breathing. He grabbed his head with his hands, and tottered over to the edge.

And from there he jumped quietly.

On Nigambodh ghat, Chandrakant set fire to his son Suri's body. After the flames rose and began engulfing the body, I turned away.

An old fakir was sitting a little distance behind us, wrapped up tight under a dirty, old, torn, bed sheet. It had been a cold December, and all of North India was under a cold snap that had already killed a handful of poor people. The old fakir was shivering.

It was the same old fakir Chandrakant and I had met years earlier in the Hazarat Nizammuddin dargah near the shrine to the first Hindi poet, Amir Khusrau, a fakir whose eyes were red like an ant's, whom the almighty did not bless with the ability to sleep, who carried thirty times its own weight its whole life.

He noticed me staring at him and got up to leave. I saw that his head was proportionally much larger than his body – something he was always trying to hide with that torn old bedsheet.

FINALLY AN ASSESSMENT BY THE WHO; A PAGE FROM
SURYAKANT'S DIARY; THE PENTAGON

Suri – Suryakant – was born sometime in September, 1995, and died on 25 December, 2004, at 12:04. He was born in a private hospital called Kalpana Health Centre between Model Town and Adarsh Nagar, but determining the exact date is no easy task, because a restaurant, day spa, and massage parlour now stand where the hospital used to be. Nobody has any idea what happened to Kalpana Health Centre. People had of course heard of the big scandal and police raid a couple years ago that had made the TV news after the kidney of an indigent man had been removed and sold.

I couldn't be sure whether nine months before his birth in that hospital when Suryakant came into his mother's womb was the time of the magic carpet, the one Chandrakant and Shobha had brought with them to the half flat of house number E-3/1, bylane number seven, Jahangirpuri, Delhi, after fleeing Sarini, and had put on the floor, and played the game they played for years to put out the fire; or whether it was true that one night he crawled like a turtle out of the dirty drainage sewer and silently entered his mother's womb that way. And the disease that made his head grow and grow, day by day, the disease the doctors said would give him a life span of two years max, the disease that had no trace in any of the medical literature, the disease Chandrakant and Shobha called 'Mangosil' but it was really only Suri who knew about the virus that caused it – it wasn't the disease that caused his death.

He himself chose when to end his life.

Suri's notebook lies open in front me at page fifty-six. He had copied down some lines of a poem in his beautiful handwriting:

> *You are still alive, you are not alone yet –*
> *She is still beside you, with her empty hands,*
> *And joy reaches you both across immense places,*
> *Through mists and hunger and flying snow,*
> *Miserable is the man who runs from a dog in his darkness…*
> *And pitiful is the one who holds out his rag of life*
> *To beg mercy of the darkness.*

I did the translation in a rush because in front of me are this year's findings from a World Health Organization report. It contains alarming statistics about millions of children in the developing countries who will fall victim to deadly diseases because of malnutrition, poverty, and squalor.

The report also included startling information about children who have been falling victim to an illness for the past several years that causes the head to grow significantly faster than the rest of the body, causing unnatural behavior. According to doctors, the virus or causes of the disease have yet to be identified, but children who suffer from this disease usually only live to two. According to the WHO, this disease, like AIDS, is spreading rapidly.

But the strangest part of the report came from the Pentagon. A total of sixty seven countries including Ethiopia, Ghana, India, Bangladesh, Iraq, Afghanistan, Bosnia, Palestine, Kosovo, Sri Lanka, Namibia, Nicaragua, and Brazil were home to children who had been born with heads that so quickly got bigger.

And they were even being born in wealthy, developed countries like the US, France, and the UK.

The brains of these children knew everything. They weren't innocent and wide-eyed like most kids.

The brains of these children were several times bigger than normal for their biological age. And several centuries of living memories were present inside these brains – you could call it a mini flash drive with all history up to the present day. Their DNA was eerily alike.

The Pentagon urged all governments of all countries to keep a close eye on these big-headed kids.

This is how they can be identified:

'They are in squalor to poor families. Their eyes are red like the eyes of ants. They more or less never sleep. And it is possible they know everything.'

TRANSLATOR'S
AFTERWORD

Life was getting better for Uday Prakash when I first met him face-to-face in August, 2005. His 'Mohandas' had just been published by the leading Hindi literary magazine *Hans*, and it was clear that the novella, to steal a phrase from Bollywood, was a superhit. The mobile numbers and postal addresses of Hindi writers are a standard part of back-flap bios in India, just in case readers would like to call and compliment the author on a job well done. And so in the car on the way back from New Delhi's Indira Gandhi International Airport to his home in nearby Ghaziabad, Prakash received call after call and SMS after SMS from happy fans who wanted to tell him how much they'd enjoyed reading the story. He continually pulled the car over to receive felicitations from a local colleague, or a stranger from elsewhere. Things were changing quickly in India, as Prakash often points out in his stories – and one advantage of mass mobile-phone ownership, if nothing else, has been that lonely poets and writers are able to receive at least a little boost now and again from their readers.

When he and I had first emailed a couple of years earlier about my translating his novel *The Girl with the Golden Parasol* (Penguin India, 2008), I had little idea about the 'dark days,' as Prakash puts it, he was passing through – a period in his life he alludes to at least once in all three stories of this volume. Prakash has always been a popular writer with a huge base of readers: before mobiles, and even in 2005, he received stacks of one-rupee postcards every day from admirers spread across the most forgotten corners of India. (After the publication of 'Mohandas,' many postcards simply read, 'I am Mohandas.')

Despite his huge, grass-roots fan base, Prakash has always had an uneasy relationship with the Hindi establishment, or any other (in a phrase he likes to use) 'power centre.' For most of his professional life, he has worked as a freelance writer, journalist, poet, critic, film maker and producer: anything to provide for his family, at the mercy of the kindness of assignments, rarely able to enjoy the stability that an academic job or government post would have provided. Accused of stirring up caste unrest, called a 'rabid dog,' Prakash sustained many attacks from both left and right after the publication of *The Girl with the Golden Parasol* in 2001 (the novel tells the story of a non-Brahmin boy who falls in love with a Brahmin girl). The plug was pulled overnight on nearly all his freelance jobs. The dark days had begun – and only began to lift years later after the publication of 'Mohandas' and the winning of a PEN American Center Translation Fund Award for *The Girl with the Golden Parasol* in translation.

Uday Prakash was born on New Year's Day, 1952, in Sitapur, a village on the Son river in the state of Madhya Pradesh. Hindi is his second language: he grew up speaking Chhattisgarhi, a regional language of north India now with its own state, Chhattisgarh. His family were thakurs, or landlords of the village, in a system that was, and is, quite feudal. I have seen Prakash regale a wide-eyed five-year-old in San Francisco with the true tale of the pet elephant he called his companion as a child – and how the elephant used to assist in bathing the young writer with its trunk. Prakash's own childhood is filled with astonishingly detailed memories of close friends from the village, and the surrounding forest he used to explore – much of which has been decimated after years of deforestation, development, and the forcing off the land of indigenous inhabitants.

Prakash's mother, Ganga Devi, had come from a Bhojpuri-speaking area near Mirzapur, and had brought with her not only many Bhojpuri songs she often sang at home, but also a facility and abiding love for traditional drawings and illustrations from her region. She painted on the walls and sketched in a notebook she'd kept since she was a teenager. She was skillful, and her art made a deep impression on Prakash, the youngest of her four children, to whom she was very close. After suffering from tracheal cancer, she died two days before Prakash's thirteenth birthday.

Prakash's father was an avid reader, had a good education for the time, subscribed to many Hindi magazines, and wrote poetry – all of which spurred Prakash's own reading and writing habits. After the death of Prakash's mother, his father began drinking heavily, and it soon became difficult for Prakash to stay at home. Prakash was taken in by a teacher at a nearby town, Shahdol, sixty kilometres away: a tiny hamlet by Indian standards, but as big and strange as a foreign country to Prakash. In an age with bad roads and few bridges, it was quite far from home. He considers the teacher who looked after him a second father, and credits him for helping to guide his studies.

Prakash's father later developed carcinomas on his cheek and mouth, and Prakash travelled and stayed with him in the city of Indore as he underwent treatment. Before slipping into a coma, his father wrote a letter to a relative, kept by Prakash's youngest sister, about his fears of what would happen to Prakash. His father was worried that his son lacked sensibility in the ways of the world, and would face terrible problems in the future.

When Prakash's father died in September 1969, he left to study at the university in Sagar, Madhya Pradesh, and later, in 1975, just after the Emergency period began, moved to New Delhi where he soon began teaching comparative literature and Hindi at Jawaharlal Nehru University. For the next thirty years, he rarely travelled back home. Only recently has Prakash begun returning to Sitapur for longer periods in order spend time with his relatives and childhood friends.

'The Walls of Delhi' and 'Mangosil' – the two 'city stories' in this collection – are clearly the work of a writer who has trod extensively through the bylanes of India's sprawling capital. Still, Prakash shines greatly in his village stories. His poem *Tibet,* which earned him a prestigious poetry prize at a young age, was inspired by the chanting of Tibetan monks resettled near his village after fleeing the Chinese invasion. 'Heeralal's Ghost,' expertly translated by Robert Hueckstedt, is a fable of a low-caste servant of the village landowner who dies from overwork, then returns as a ghost to terrorise his former employer's family in episodes both hysterical and tragic. And here, in 'Mohandas,' Prakash provides a harrowing portrayal of the caste dynamics and corruption that are still a powerful force in India.

After Prakash picked me up from the airport on that sticky monsoon night in 2005, we spent a week in New Delhi discussing the translation of *The Girl with the Golden Parasol*. We also spent half a day with his longtime Hindi publisher drinking some twenty cups of tea while in tense negotiations over a decade's worth of unpaid book royalties. Prakash and I then packed up the car for the three-day trip to Sitapur. From there, we had been invited to the inauguration of a museum in the capital of Chhattisgarh, Rajnandgaon, to be dedicated in part to one of the most important twentieth-century Hindi poets, Muktibodh – a favourite of Prakash's, and a fellow struggler. At first, Prakash was reluctant to accept the invitation, since the museum and ceremony and publicity all fell under the auspices of the right-wing BJP state government of Chhattisgarh; the Chief Minister of the state – by coincidence, a distant relation of Prakash's – would be cutting the ribbon. In the end, Prakash decided that it was more important to support recognition of Muktibodh, a man marginalised in his own time, than to keep away from politics he disagreed with.

Muktibodh is the name of the independent-minded judge in 'Mohandas,' and we were joined on the trip to Rajnandgaon by Virendra Soni, to whom the story is dedicated. So I suppose I shouldn't have been surprised that as we were leaving town, Prakash, seeing a man on the road walking toward us, said, 'Oh, there's Mohandas.' And so it was: the man who he had based his character on, looking just as haggard and resilient as described in the story. We stopped, spoke at length, took some photos and went on.

Our host for the festivities was the district collector of Rajnandgaon, who put us up in VIP accommodations at a local chicken magnate's bungalow. The next day Prakash and other guests read from their work. I will never forget the hundreds of Prakash's young fans who, hearing he would be in attendance, had travelled long distances and made huge sacrifices to see him in person. In particular, I remember one young man who was unable to walk being carried by four of his friends into the hall. 'These are my readers,' Prakash told me.

Though we had assumed that we would attend the museum dedication as spectators, an assistant the next day informed us we would share a dais with the Chief Minister, and that we would be flower-garlanded on stage. In one of the more terrifying moments of my life, once on stage I was instructed to give a speech in Hindi to the thousands assembled. The Chief Minister, speaking last, wasted no time in transforming the oddity of a Hindi-speaking American into political gain: 'The Congress party may have Sonia Gandhi,' he told the crowd. 'But we have Jason! And his Hindi is better than hers.' 'We're here for Muktibodh,' Prakash whispered to me by way of reassurance after the ribbon-cutting.

In many of his stories, Uday Prakash shows how those who dare to dissent against a suffocating system are punished. But with his biting satire and delightful narrative detours he also demonstrates how humor and compassion ultimately provide the best means to fight back and escape. These two elements combine in stories that are like a mix of Milan Kundera blended with *Tristram Shandy* — and told by one of the most naturally gifted storytellers writing in any language. Among Hindi writers, Prakash has broken from a strict model of social realism that dominated Hindi fiction for much of the twentieth-century, though he maintains many satirical elements of writers like Manohar Shyam Joshi, while inventing a humor that is all his own. As one prominent Hindi literary critic recently told me, 'Uday Prakash is knocking on the canon.' As he continues to knock, he has already spawned a cottage industry of young imitators.

After the publication of 'Mohandas' and *The Girl with the Golden Parasol,* and later, when the Indian national literary body, the Sahitya Akademi, awarded Uday Prakash its highest honour in Hindi for 'Mohandas,' and *Kindle* magazine named him a top South Asian youth icon, the dark days began to recede. Life for Uday Prakash as an independent Hindi writer continues to be difficult and uncertain, but less so. It is his hope to spend much of his time writing in relative peace possibly in Berlin, where his son, daughter-in-law, and grandson live. He is currently at work on several projects, among them a novel entitled *Cheena Baba* about a Chinese soldier who deserts during the 1962 Indo-China war and makes his home in a tree near the Indian border with Nepal.

I have followed a couple of basic strategies in translating these three stories. First, I have tried to make Prakash's prose sound as contemporary and relevant in English as it does in Hindi without, I hope, sounding over colloquial or slangy. Second, I have attempted to render his prose into an English that is both readable and comprehensible by English speakers not only from the Indian subcontinent, but also from Australia, the US, the UK, and elsewhere. Translators from Hindi and other South Asian languages into English face a problem that translators from, say, French or Spanish don't have to grapple with. South Asian English can differ in many meaningful ways from the way English is spoken and written in other parts of the world. In addition, English speakers from the Indian subcontinent can usually be expected to understand the cultural context of the stories more readily than someone from Oklahoma or Alice Springs might. Hindi and Indian words, too, from *adivasi* (a tribal or aboriginal) to *zamindar* (landowner) would probably need no explanation: if I had been translating exclusively for an Indian audience, the temptation would have been to leave Hindi words like this 'as is,' even in the English. But one of the goals of translating is to enlarge the conversation, and conversations don't work if someone feels left out. Therefore, keeping in mind that the readers of this book will come from a variety of English backgrounds, I have assumed little or no prior knowledge of India or Hindi. In the few instances I have decided to retain words like *adivasi* or *zamindar*, I have inserted a brief gloss within the text that should provide readers with sufficient clues as to the meaning. Or, I've concluded that enough context already exists for the reader to understand the meaning, if not the gist, of the word or phrase. (I prefer this solution to footnotes or glossaries, which I avoid, since they are not found in the Hindi, and I believe they can give the story an unwanted and unnecessary air of academic writing.) At the same time, I have tried to avoid 'pre-chewing' the text too much for South Asians who may be, at least culturally, closer to the Hindi. My greatest hope is that at least some of the enormous pleasure I took in translating these wonderful stories, and the important voice of Uday Prakash, is evident in the English.

ABOUT THE AUTHOR

UDAY PRAKASH is a major voice of contemporary Hindi literature. His works of fiction and poetry published over the past twenty-five years, which have earned him Indian and international literary awards and are translated into ten languages. Also a filmmaker and playwright, Prakash divides his time between New Delhi and Sitapur in Madhya Pradesh.

ABOUT THE TRANSLATOR

Translator JASON GRUNEBAUM is senior lecturer in Hindi at the University of Chicago, where he also teaches creative writing.

ABOUT SEVEN STORIES PRESS